HIS THIRD VICTIM

A gripping crime thriller full of twists

HELEN H. DURRANT

Published 2017 by Joffe Books, London.

www.joffebooks.com

This book is a work of fiction. Names, characters, businesses, organizations, places and events are either the product of the author's imagination or are used fictitiously. Any resemblance to actual persons, living or dead, events or locales is entirely coincidental. The spelling is British English.

ISBN- 978-1-912106-19-6

For my husband Peter, who has been exploring the Pennine villages with me for years.

Prologue

He swiped his finger across the screen of his mobile and screwed up his eyes. What he saw made him feel sick. Bella Richards had a new man in her life. He'd videoed Bella and this Alan Fisher fawning over each other, her fingers stroking Fisher's cheek, her lips on his mouth.

She was wasting her time. Bella was no good for Fisher or anyone else. Why didn't she learn? Sooner or later she would go too far. If that happened, he would have to give her a scare. He knew what Bella, just like the others, was most afraid of. It hadn't been hard to work out. Very soon, and with very little effort, he would make her nightmares come true.

Alan Fisher was a complication he hadn't reckoned with. He would have to sort it. Still, it wouldn't be a problem. He was a past master at the murder game. As far as the police were aware, there had been five so far. Alan Fisher would simply be added to the list.

What the police didn't know was that the five were nothing but collateral damage. They were people who got in the way and had to disappear because they were too close to his *real* targets. The police had no idea about those. That was because he was clever and meticulous. His 'perfect crimes' had gone completely unnoticed. No one had even reported the women missing.

He had been praying that Bella might be different. The other two hadn't lived up to expectations. So he had had to kill them. He now had Bella in his sights, and it would be nice if she didn't become his third victim. All she had to do was make him happy. It wasn't much to ask, but his chosen ones always seemed to fail him in one way or another. All the same, he persisted in his search. One day he would find a woman who would live up to his dreams. He hoped that Bella was the one.

Chapter 1

Day 1

The policeman dashed into Victoria Station, flashed his badge at the man on the barrier, and ran straight to platform four. He scanned the crowds waiting for the Huddersfield train. There they were. A man and a woman, arm in arm. They were a good-looking couple. Alan Fisher was tall, dark and expensively dressed, with an athletic build. Bella Richards was a slim, petite blonde, her chin-length hair swishing about her delicate features. She took his hand and tried to pull him towards the waiting train.

"Alan Fisher?" the policeman said with some urgency.

Fisher nodded.

"I need you to come with me at once. It's your wife." The policeman watched Fisher's look of surprise quickly turned to shock. All sorts of possibilities would be raging through his mind.

"Why? What's the problem?" Fisher asked.

"I don't have any details, sir. I've been told to pick you up and take you straight to Huddersfield Infirmary." Easily said, but the words implied the worst.

"Is Anna alright? Has she had an accident? Is she ill?"

The policeman shook his head. "Like I said, sir, I haven't been told anything." His eyes flicked to the station clock. "We should get going."

"I'll ring the house first," Fisher said firmly.

The policeman saw the suspicion in Fisher's eyes and didn't like it.

"There is no one there. I believe the lady who does your cleaning has gone with her." The words had the right effect. Reassured, Fisher turned to his companion.

"I'll have to go. Get on the train. I'll ring you later." He bent down and kissed her cheek.

The policeman took Fisher's arm. "My car is outside. We should get going. The traffic's bad at this time of day."

Moments later they were driving along the Ashton Road.

Alan Fisher tapped his fingers on his knees and looked at the officer. "Wouldn't the motorway be better? There must be a holdup somewhere — the traffic is at a standstill."

"I'll pick it up at Stockport," the policeman assured him.

"Has Anna had an accident? She wasn't driving, was she?"

"I've no idea, sir."

"Can't you find out? You know, get on the radio? Ask someone?"

"Be patient, you'll be there shortly."

The traffic was moving at a snail's pace. For as far as they could see ahead, vehicles were doing nothing more than crawling along. Suddenly the officer pulled off the main road and into one of the dozens of backstreets. It was narrow, bordered on both sides by red-brick terraced houses. "Shortcut." He smiled at Fisher.

"Are you sure?" Fisher sounded doubtful. "I thought there was nothing down here but the canal."

"I know a shortcut onto the Rochdale Road. From there we'll pick up the M60 then the M62."

But Fisher was right. The narrow side street came to an abrupt end at a canal footbridge that no cars could cross. The only thing separating them from the water were rusted iron railings.

"What are you doing?" Fisher's doubt had now turned to annoyance. The policeman ignored his words. It was to be expected. "We'll waste even more time going back."

"It doesn't matter now, sir. This is as far as we go."

The look of confusion on Alan Fisher's face made the policeman smile. He loved winding them up.

"This isn't right. This is some sort of scam. Who are you?" Fisher demanded.

The policeman didn't reply. He was busy rifling around in the glove box. He knew the man was losing patience and he needed to act quickly. A few seconds later, he was pointing a loaded pistol at Fisher's temple.

"Say goodbye."

There could be no doubt or confusion now. The look of horror on Fisher's face was swiftly replaced by the determination to save himself. The "officer" dodged the first blow. Fisher lunged forward with his fist again. Too late. The "policeman" pulled the trigger, and that was the end of Fisher.

Chapter 2

It was the middle of the night. The only light came from a moon that occasionally wandered out from behind thick cloud. It was cold too, which was only to be expected up here in early spring.

The top of the moor was a bleak spot even on a good day. But at night it was the last place anyone would choose to be. The police car had pulled up at the side of a narrow road that twisted its way between the Saddleworth villages and those on the outskirts of Huddersfield. The body lay beneath a makeshift tent a few metres away.

The headlights of a second car could be seen in the distance, coming closer. One of the uniformed officers turned to his colleague. "Bennett."

"Hope so, then perhaps we can get out of here. My feet are like ice."

DI George Bennett worked for Manchester Central. He'd been told about the body and decided to attend. He could have left it to Oldham, but from the initial report it had all the hallmarks of a gangland killing.

He got out of his car and pulled aside the tent flap. "Who found it?"

"A bloke from the village down there. Picked up the shape in the headlights of his car. Rang it in, left his number, then did one."

"Find him, ask if he saw anyone else, or any other traffic on this road. Do we know who the victim is?"

"His wallet and phone are still on him, sir. He's Alan Fisher, a lecturer from a college in Huddersfield. There's about a hundred quid in the wallet, so it wasn't robbery."

"Pathologist on his way?"

"I rang it in to Oldham. I presume they're sending someone out, but it is tricky to find it if you don't know this area."

Bennett looked around him at the bleak moorland. Wasn't that the truth!

"This could be him now, sir."

Another car was coming along the road, this time from the Yorkshire side. It stopped in front of Bennett's car and two men got out.

* * *

"Trying to make off with our body, are you?" The voice boomed loud through the darkness. "Hope you lot haven't touched owt that'll bugger up forensics."

Detective Superintendent Talbot Dyson was a big man in his early fifties. He was overweight and his facial features didn't sit comfortably together. Some would describe him as downright ugly, but there was something about him that made him likeable, even attractive. He was always impeccably dressed. Tonight he was in a grey suit, and a three-quarter length overcoat, with a silk scarf around his neck. He walked towards Bennett and the uniforms flashing his ID, while his colleague went into the tent to look at the body.

"You have no right here. This one is ours," Bennett shouted.

Dyson smiled. "I think you'll find it's mine. I've got help coming, so we'll have this road cleared for you very soon."

"No you don't, Superintendent. This man died on our side of the fence. This is our case. Get your man out of that tent, or there will be nothing left for forensics to find."

Dyson folded his arms. "This is not a crime scene. It's merely the dump site."

"Whatever it is, leave it to us."

Dyson pointed. "Look over there. What do you see?"

"Road signs. So what?"

"That one there says we're in Greater Manchester, which was in Lancashire last I looked. T'other, across from it, says we're in West Yorkshire. The smart-arse has left him placed half and half, right between the two. He's playing us, Inspector."

Bennet lowered his voice. "I suspect that this is a gangland murder. You must have heard about the trouble we've had since Ron Chalker was put away? Every villain in Greater Manchester is reaching for the crown. A bastard I've been after for months is probably responsible for this killing. That body could hold the proof I need."

Dyson stepped away from him. "It won't, and you're wrong." He turned to his inspector. "Well?"

"He's ours, sir. Pistol shot to the head and he's got the mark."

Dyson sighed. "What bloody colour this time?"

"Blue, sir."

"Mark? What mark?" Bennett frowned.

"On his forearm. A round mark made by a rubber stamp. The type kids get when they go to gigs and the like."

"Still doesn't make him yours."

Dyson was trying to be patient. "I think it does, and for two very good reasons, Inspector. For starters, most of him is lying on the West Yorkshire side. Plus, over the last three years we've had five others with marks on their arms just like his lying in the morgue in Huddersfield."

Chapter 3

Dyson walked into the largest of the three morgues at Pennine Forensics. The forensic pathology unit was attached to Huddersfield Infirmary and provided services for the East Pennine police.

"What have you got for me, Sid?"

"Give us a chance, Talbot. He wasn't brought in until the early hours."

They had worked together on dozens of cases over the years and knew each other well. Professor Sid Bibby was the same age as the super. What was left of his hair was grey, but unlike Talbot, he took care of himself, and maintained a healthy weight.

Dyson stood over the body of Alan Fisher, picking at his teeth. "Is it the same killer, or what? You'll know that by now, surely. I've got a team back at the nick kicking their heels. Need summat to throw 'em."

"Talbot, watch what you're doing." Professor Bibby shoved the weighty superintendent out of the way. "We're running tests on the bullet. It was a .22, fired from a small pistol, same as the others. He was shot in the temple. I'd say the muzzle was held against the skin. See, the entrance wound is surrounded by a wide area of soot, and the skin is seared and blackened."

"Anything else?"

"The mark you know about. He had a dodgy gall bladder, but apart from that, he was in perfect health. I'll run the usual tests for drugs etc. Not that I expect to find anything."

"Did you find anything that'll help us nail the killer? You know, fibres on the clothes? A smear of blood? The way things are right now, I'd settle for a speck of dust."

"Tests on his clothing are ongoing, but if this killing follows the pattern of the others, then I wouldn't hold out any hope."

Dyson walked across to the window. "Why the gap? It's been over a year since the last one. Where's the bastard been? What's he been doing?"

"Not killing random people, so we should be thankful," Sid chipped in.

But Dyson had never thought the killings were random. He'd nothing to back that up other than his gut, and the marks on their arms. He was sure the colour of the mark was significant too.

"We've had three green, and two red. Now the bugger's going for blue. Anything fresh on the ink?"

"You'll have to give me more time. I should have something definite for you by tomorrow. I am going to release the body now. We've got everything we need."

Dyson gave a weary sigh. "Okay, I'll trouble you no more. I'll go and see what I can prise out of my lacklustre team. I keep waiting for one of them to suggest talking to the woman who was with Fisher at the station. Apart from the killer, she was the last person to see him alive."

Sid chuckled. "They can't be that bad, surely?"

"Oh they are. Doing my bloody head in, the pair of 'em."

Dyson currently had Frank Carlisle as his DI. He had been transferred from Halifax, with DC Ian Beckwith in tow. Neither had much to recommend them. Carlisle liked the easy life, and Beckwith was still green around the gills. What Dyson wanted — no, what he *needed* — was DI Matt Brindle back.

* * *

Despite the bleakness of the spot, and the fact that it was only a day old, the place where Fisher's body had been found had become a shrine. Tributes to the popular lecturer were piled at the side of the narrow country road. The police tent had gone, and there wasn't a uniformed officer in sight. All that remained was an assortment of expensive blooms, wrapped in ribbon and bearing words of sympathy.

He cleared his throat and spat onto the ground. What a waste of money. Alan Fisher had had to die. There was no other way — he was too close to Bella. People knew they had been seeing each other. Once she disappeared, Fisher would have been questioned. Plus, the man had promised Bella a future. That was not allowed, so he had paid the price.

The subject of all these tributes had turned her head with promises he could not keep. Stupid fool! Bella's future wasn't with Fisher. And preparations were well in hand. He smiled. Bella was slim, blonde, and she had the finest skin — pale, clear, and set off with the most amazing bright blue eyes. Spending time with her would be no burden at all.

He knelt down and began picking up the bouquets and balloons one by one. They had been left by friends, colleagues and students from his college. The man read each card in turn before roughly tossing it to the ground. Finally he spotted what he'd been looking for. Her tribute was an arrangement of red roses. He leaned forward and snatched it up. The card caught his attention immediately. The message was simple: "To my one true love, yours forever, Bella."

Slut! Why have you spoiled things? Sure, leave flowers if you want. That's expected. They had worked together. The soppy words tore at his soul and he ripped the card from the bouquet. She was deluding herself. She had not loved Alan Fisher. He put the card in his pocket. He would make her eat those words.

Fisher's death was progress. It should have made him feel better. But it hadn't worked, and now he felt worse. Bella's life had continued as before. She was still living in the same house, still working at the same job. His mind was in turmoil, so full of fear and hate that it literally gave him a headache. He must act. She needed a further lesson, something sharp and painful. Something soul destroying and so dreadful that it would jolt her to her senses.

Chapter 4

Day 6

Bella played with the heart-shaped locket around her neck. She watched Matt Brindle pour a generous slug of red wine into his glass, before topping up hers.

He smiled. "I hate these things. Funerals are all strangers and tears. Give me a wedding any day."

"Doesn't that make them much the same thing?" Bella spoke absently, gazing into space.

"On that level, yes, but the atmosphere is very different. Did you know Alan well?"

Bella gave the room a quick scan. *How many people here know the truth?* "Did you?" she asked, deflecting the question.

Brindle shook his head. "I met him when I did the London Marathon last year, and again on the Manchester run. We got on. We emailed a little. Alan was a computer nerd. He helped me set up a small network for my home office. You?"

She had never met Brindle before, but he'd been at her side from the moment they left the church. Bella put it down to his not knowing anyone here. Or was there another reason for his clinging to her like this? Was he trying to chat her up? Bella couldn't be sure. But if he was, she had to put a stop to it. The last thing she needed or wanted right now was a romance. Apart from friendly chatter, she'd given him no encouragement. What was it Alan used to say? That she attracted men like flies round a jam pot. Bella felt the tears well up again. Thinking of Alan, and how she would miss him, was so painful it cut into her very soul.

Though Brindle would definitely get her aunt's seal of approval, something Alan never had. Him being married had put paid to that. This man was every bit as good-looking as Alan, even if he did have some sort of injury. Brindle limped. It was only slight, as if something were slightly out of sync. Bella had watched him walk, and the leg was obviously painful. More than once this afternoon she'd caught him rubbing his thigh and wincing. The rest of him wasn't bad, but his dark hair looked as if it had recently suffered at the hands of an overenthusiastic barber. It was a shame because a better hair cut would balance his nose, which was slightly too long. Physically, he was much the same size and build as Alan. Over six foot, and wiry. He looked like an athlete, though she couldn't think how he managed with that leg. She wouldn't ask though. It might make him think she was interested, and she wasn't. It was just idle curiosity, something to distract from the horror of what had happened to Alan. A wandering mind staved off the awful reality and she was grateful for the diversion.

"I worked with that computer nerd." The last thing Bella wanted today was small talk, but there was no avoiding it. These were Alan's friends and colleagues, some of them hers too. And they were in his home. "In fact, most of the people here worked with him. We were both lecturers at the local college, in the IT department."

"So he was a colleague."

"And a friend, and recently . . ." she paused. The lump in her throat was back, and the tears welled again. *Admit the truth. Let this man know where he stands.* "Recently we'd become lovers."

Brindle coughed. "How did that go down with . . . with his wife?"

Bella tried to smile, adopt a casual tone, but it was hard. Not because of the wife, but because this was Alan she was talking about. He had been the man she loved, the man she hoped to spend the rest of her life with. There was nothing casual in that. "They were practically separated." Her voice was thin and strained. "And before you even start to question that, I didn't cause their marriage to break down. It was over long before we got together. This is a big house. Although they both lived here, Alan had his own space."

Brindle looked at her. "Even so, why not simply move out? Anna couldn't have been happy to have him here while he was seeing you."

Was that a criticism? Did all the folk here think the same? Did they think that in the last few months, Alan still held out hope for his marriage?" Why had she been so open to a complete stranger? Grief, that was why. Her head was in turmoil. No way would she ordinarily discuss her love life with someone she had never met before.

Her voice was flat. "It was down to finances and negotiating a settlement. But recently Alan had inherited some money from his father. His problem sorted, he was about to move in with me. Half his stuff is at my place already." A chill had crept into Bella's tone. People were so quick to judge. "The truth is, the marriage was over. There is nothing more to say."

Brindle nodded. "He did say that Anna was a difficult woman. Apparently it was her money that bought this place. She was from a well-heeled family. I picked up on the fact that that he and Anna weren't happy. He also told me how possessive she was. Leaving her would have demanded the kid glove treatment." He paused. "Look — I'm sorry. This must be difficult for you. I had no idea you and Alan . . ."

"No reason you should. We kept things quiet."

Bella smiled at him. Matt Brindle had known Alan. It was natural he should be curious, question her motives. But it made her think.

"The way he died, do you know what happened?" he asked.

"We were together on Victoria Station in Manchester when the policeman came to get him. Said there was a problem with Anna. No one has explained anything to me, but I know they found his body up on the moors." Her voice faltered. She'd heard the news on the local radio. Alan had been shot through the head. It made no sense. She could only guess at what had happened to him when he'd left Victoria. Alan had no enemies. She presumed he'd been the victim of a mugging gone wrong.

"You were with him."

She looked away. This wasn't what she wanted to talk about. The day was difficult enough. She had precious little to offer anyway. Bella dipped her head. Earlier she'd had the tears under control. "I'm sorry. I can't do this. It's all too raw."

"My fault. I shouldn't have brought it up. And I should have at least explained. It's in my nature to be nosey, to ask questions. I used to be with the police — with East Pennine CID in fact."

Bella was glad of the change of subject. She had been on the point of embarrassing herself by dissolving into tears again. "Used to be? You gave it up?"

"I left the force six months ago."

"Do you miss it?" she asked.

"Whether I miss it or not isn't the issue. All I ever wanted to do was to work in CID, but a nasty incident put paid to that." He tapped his leg. "Shattered. It's full of metal now."

She made no comment.

"Do you know him?" Brindle nodded at a tall, thin man who was standing on the other side of the room, staring at them.

"He's a colleague from work." Bella gave the man a wave. "I'd better go and have a word. He will be as much in the dark as me." Giving Brindle a half-hearted smile, Bella made her way over to him.

"Joel, you made it."

He kissed her cheek. "I'm sorry. Bella, I know how you felt about Alan. This must be killing you."

"It's so hard, and I really am struggling. I can't believe he's gone." The tears ran freely down her cheeks. No need to stand on ceremony with Joel.

Joel Dawson offered her a tissue and put his arm around her shoulder. "We'll all miss him."

Bella gave him a wan smile. Like her, Joel was a relatively new member of the department, but he fitted in well. Both staff and students liked him. He was a quiet, unassuming, kindly man, but nonetheless the type folk never really got to know.

Still sobbing, she shook her head. "I can't do this, Joel. I'm going outside to get some air. I'm better off on my own." Leaving Joel Dawson staring after her, Bella moved towards the French doors and the garden beyond. She wanted to take a look at the place where Alan had lived, and this was her only chance. He'd talked about the house, but she'd never been here. It wouldn't have been right. He and Anna might be finished, but Bella had no desire to rub her nose in it. But that didn't stop her being curious.

"Beautiful garden. All Anna's work. Alan wasn't one for gardening."

A man she hadn't spoken to yet had followed her out. He'd thrown a smile her way once or twice during the service, but Bella had ignored him. He was tall and wore an well-cut dark suit.

He stood beside her. "He loved this house. That's why his wife agreed to have the wake here. In the evenings Alan used to sit on the bench over there." He pointed to a shady corner. "He'd drink wine and work until Anna gave up on the nagging and went to bed."

"Why isn't she here?" An obvious enough question, but she could see that it made the man uncomfortable. Despite their problems, Anna was still legally Alan's wife, and this was his funeral. Bella didn't think the question out of turn. Everyone here must be wondering the same thing.

He pulled a face and shrugged his broad shoulders. "Anna couldn't face it. Sent the family solicitor instead. Me." He gave her a big smile. "I'm Robert Nolan. I'm also a neighbour — I live over there." He pointed to the huge hedge between this and the nearest house.

"Bella Richards. Alan and I worked together." She looked up at him. *Did he know?* "Maybe Alan told you about me?"

Robert nodded and gave her another smile. "He loved you. I know that much."

"And I loved him back. We had made plans. If he hadn't . . . died," she closed her eyes, "We would have been going away for a holiday this week."

He gave a long whistle. "This will have hit you hard."

"I don't think I've ever been so miserable. It might help if I knew what happened. But no one has told me, and I don't feel I have the right to ask."

He was looking at her, his eyes dark and troubled. "Alan was shot, deliberately executed. His body was found dumped on a moorland road."

The world around her was suddenly silent. His words thundered in her head. *That can't be right. Who would want to kill Alan?* Her fingers reached for the locket again. Alan's last gift to her. The words were stark, cold. She didn't, *couldn't* believe them.

After a while she managed to speak again. "Who would want to do that? And why? What for?"

"The police are on it. I'm surprised they haven't spoken to you. You do know that you're the main beneficiary of Alan's will?"

Bella turned away. She'd forgotten. Given the circumstances, the fact embarrassed her.

Chapter 5

Day 8

Two days had passed since the funeral, and Bella was back at college. She hadn't wanted to return to work. It was tedious now, had lost something. She was utterly miserable. Her thoughts kept straying to Alan, and the life they could have had together.

Kate Hathershaw strode into the IT department staffroom, and announced, "Them upstairs want our student progression data."

Bella sighed. She was tired and had hoped for an early finish. "It makes you wonder if they really know our students. My lot this year are nothing but a load of trainee villains. In fact, never mind the data, I've a good mind to take the front page of the *Chronicle* with me. Four of them were sent down last month."

Kate grinned. "Go on — dare you! I'd love to see old 'Brainstorm's' face."

Brainstorm was a nickname Alan had given to a member of the college senior management team. It reflected his constant push for new ideas, and innovative ways of persuading the area's youth to beat a path to their door.

Bella's tears threatened to spill again. Alan's desk had faced hers, and when they were both working in the staffroom she could look up and catch his eye. Now his desk had been cleared, ready for its new occupant. Bella had emptied the drawers, making sure there was nothing personal for any snoopers to find. She and Alan used to write little notes to each other. She didn't want a colleague finding one.

"Joel was wondering if he could have Alan's desk," said Kate.

Bella frowned. Could she stand looking at Joel, day after day, and know that he was looking back at her? The thought made her shudder. Alan had made coming to work every day fun. Now it was a chore. Very soon, she'd be sick of it.

"I'll have to do something about Olly." Olly was Bella's five-year-old son. "I promised I'd pick him up today." Easy to say, but not so easy to accomplish. She had not lived in the area long enough to build up a network of friends, or know other mums who could look after him for a short time. She checked the contacts on her phone. Her regular minder had a hospital appointment. That left no one, well no one she would ordinarily trust. But today she had no choice. Bella was hoping for promotion. She could do with the money, so missing meetings wasn't a good idea. It was all very well that Alan had left her a small fortune in his will, but his wife would doubtless contest it. So it could be months, years even before she saw a penny.

With no one else available to pick up Olly, it would have to be her neighbour. If the woman was free that was. Desperate times, she told herself, and tapped on the number. But then how hard could it be? Olly was a good child who usually did as he was told, and the school was only a short walk from their home.

She held her breath. "Mrs Stamford, it's Bella from next door. Could you do me a huge favour? Would you pick Olly up from school for me today? I wouldn't ask but there's a meeting at work I can't get out of."

Her neighbour agreed immediately, sounding only too pleased. She told Bella she'd be at the school gate by three fifteen, and promised not to let her down.

"Keep him at yours until I get back. Don't let him play out on the street. I won't be late." She ended the call with a sigh of relief.

"Times like this a live-in partner comes in handy," Kate said wisely. "Take it from me, the voice of experience. Mike might not be up to much but he is on tap, and he loves the kids."

Bella shook her head. "Gabe left us when Olly was a baby, remember? Reckoned he couldn't hack it."

"Shame about Alan. You'd have been perfect together."

"Let it drop, Kate." But her colleague was right. Alan had no kids of his own, but he'd taken to Olly straight away, and the little boy had loved him back. She wasn't the only one who had suffered since his death. Olly was hurting too. Bella picked up her phone again. She needed to tell the school about Mrs Stamford picking up Olly. Red tape, but reassuring.

* * *

The woman was seventy, if she was a day. The boy was a delicate-looking youngster, about five years old, with blond hair like his mother's. He carried his lunch bag. He was in his school uniform: short grey trousers, a white polo shirt and a red jumper with the school logo on the sleeve. That made the man smile. Kids looked so cute at that age. Then he remembered why he was here.

The woman walked away from the school gates, the boy skipping out in front. She was carrying a shopping bag. It looked heavy. He was considering whether to pull up and offer them a lift when the woman stopped on the pavement to talk to some bloke. The boy was a few metres further on, staring in the newsagents' window.

The man drove past, parked up around the corner, and walked back.

"That's a good one." He pointed to a comic. "My lad gets it every week."

The boy looked up at him. "My mum buys mine."

His mum really should have warned him about talking to strangers. "Who are you with?"

"Mrs Stamford." He pointed to the woman. She had her back to them and was still deep in conversation with the bloke.

"I've got some comics in the boot of my car. It's only round the corner. I was taking them to recycle, but you can have them if you want." He watched the expression on the boy's face. He was considering it. Finally the lad nodded his head.

They walked away. "I like your tattoos," said the boy. "Did it hurt, when you got them?"

The man laughed and thrust his arms out in front of him so the lad could get a better look. "No, it was fine."

"What are they?"

He ran a hand down his left arm. "That's a wolf's head. And on the other there's a dragon."

"I'm going to get a snake one done when I'm older."

This was too easy. Weren't kids told not to do things like this? "Here you are." He opened the boot of his car then stepped back, looking surprised. "I must have forgotten to put them in. What am I like?" He laughed.

Oliver looked disappointed. "Doesn't matter."

"Yes, it does. I said you could have them. I know what, get in, I'll whizz you round to mine and get them for you. I'll have you back in minutes. It's only round the corner."

Stupid kid didn't even argue. He hoisted his slight frame into the passenger seat and didn't say a word. Now for the fun bit.

Chapter 6

She hadn't got over the first nightmare yet. But the one waiting for her at home was even worse. Bella returned after the meeting to find her house full of police. Mrs Stamford was sitting on the sofa, crying her eyes out.

"I was talking to Jack a second or two, no more. When I looked round, little Oliver had disappeared," she wailed.

"We're doing everything we can," the female PC told Bella. The radio on her jacket was buzzing away, and she kept touching the buttons. It was distracting. Bella couldn't take in what she was saying. It was all a jumble of words that didn't make sense. *Oliver?* Where was her child?

But the PC was still talking. "Your neighbour rang us straight away. He hasn't been gone long. Chances are he's wandered off to the park or met a friend."

"Oliver doesn't do that." The words came out of Bella's mouth sounding like someone else's. She was shaking.

"Who are Oliver's friends, Bella?" The man wasn't wearing a police uniform. There was no sympathy in his voice.

"I . . . I don't know. He's only five, he's friends with everyone." She'd meant to say everyone in his class but it had come out wrong. "Who are you?"

"I'm DC Beckwith. I'm with East Pennine CID."

CID. What on earth did they think had happened to Olly? "Where is my little boy?" The tears streamed down her cheeks. She felt faint. "Olly wouldn't just walk away. He knows we always come straight home. I've told him about wandering off, about talking to strangers."

"We have officers going over the route home, speaking to shopkeepers."

Bella felt sick. She was deathly white. The policewoman helped her to the sofa. "What do you mean? What do you think has happened to him?" Her head was spinning, full of different possibilities, all of them horrific. She turned on Mrs Stamford, her face red with sudden rage.

"Why didn't he come home with you? It's not far. Surely even you could manage that." Bella spat the words then watched the woman dissolve into tears. This was all wrong.

The policewoman put a hand on her shoulder. "Right now we're not sure what happened, Bella. We don't know if it's significant, but Oliver was seen with a man outside the newsagents. We're talking to the shop assistant now."

A stranger had taken her child. Oh God, no. Anything but that.

* * *

Oliver Richards was asleep on the passenger seat beside him. He'd given the boy a bottle of cola with something added to it. Nothing major, a sedative, but it had knocked the boy out cold.

He had left the town and driven for miles up onto the moors. By now Bella Richards would be frantic with worry. What she was going through this time would be infinitely worse than losing Alan Fisher. Her thoughts of what might be happening to her boy would be eating her raw. Served her right. Loving Fisher so much had been a mistake.

Time to get rid. He pulled off the road onto a dirt track and drove for another half a mile. He stopped outside a small cottage and turned off the engine. He went round to the passenger side and hauled the boy out. Oliver Richards hardly stirred. The man dragged him across the yard, banged on the cottage door and then dumped the kid on the step. He shivered. It was cold, and it had started to rain.

* * *

The police had appointed a family liaison officer, Alison Wray, to stay with Bella. She'd insisted that Bella went up to bed, and try and get some rest. How was she supposed to sleep? There was no way she was going to swallow the pills the doctor had left for her. She needed to be alert in case anything happened. Anyway, her head was too full of Olly. It was late now and pitch black outside. He was out there somewhere, wanting her, possibly hurting. Crying. They had a routine, the same thing every night. Bath, supper, teeth then a story in his bed. He'd snuggle in and she'd lie beside him while she read a bit more of the pirate book he liked. What was her little boy doing right this minute? Was he cold? Hungry? This was more than she could bear. If she lost Olly for good, she wouldn't want to go on. She'd rather be dead.

From time to time she heard voices downstairs, Alice talking on the phone to her colleagues. Alice was supposed to keep her up to date with events. Events! Bella sobbed into the pillow. What that meant was, if they found Olly — dead or alive. She knew they would have spoken to all his friends by now. He wasn't with any of them, so someone must have taken him.

Bella tossed and turned, torturing herself until daylight. It was no use, she couldn't lie there and do nothing. She pulled a dressing gown around her slim frame and went downstairs. Alison was dozing in the armchair. Her clothes were creased, her short hair a tousled mess.

Bella went into the kitchen. She always made herself tea and toast before calling Olly. Today she couldn't face eating anything, the thought of it made her sick. She pulled up the blind. It was raining outside. If Olly was out there in the open, he'd be wet and cold.

Alison stood at the kitchen door, stretching and yawning. "Bella, you're up. There has been a development overnight."

Bella's eyes flew to the woman's face and she tried to glean what the 'development' might be. There was no smile, Alison's expression stayed the same. So it was bad.

"We have found a bag, the type children take a packed lunch to school in."

Bella inhaled deeply. "Olly's bag has pirates on it, and it has his name inside."

"Yes, we know. The bag is his. It has been taken to our forensic people for them to look at."

Bella had so many questions, but they stuck in her throat. The answers had the power to destroy her. Still, she had to know. "Where did you find it? Was there any sign of Olly? Were there houses nearby?"

Alison spoke gently. "It was found by a member of the public. Olly's disappearance has been on the news. A woman walking her dog found it in a ditch on a road not far from the motorway."

The words hit her like a physical blow. Bella doubled up in pain. "He's dead, isn't he?" she screamed. "Some bastard has killed my little boy!"

Alison helped her to the sofa. "We don't know that. We can't presume anything. It is still early in the investigation."

The words were meant to comfort her, but they didn't. Bella howled into a cushion. She might never see Olly again, and she couldn't bear it.

Chapter 7

Day 9

It was early, just after dawn. Matt Brindle woke with a start. His eyes were wide open, and a cold sweat blanketed his body.

His demons were back. The nightmare had returned and served up another bad night.

He sat up, rubbed at his head and looked around the room. Everything was exactly as it should be. He wasn't in that building. No one had tried to blow him up. All that had happened to another man, in another time. He was at home, in his own bed, exhausted but whole. In body, at least. He wasn't so sure about his mind. He steadied his breathing. Six months had passed, but the effects of that day's trauma hadn't dissipated.

His mother came into the room without knocking. "Coffee and the paper. The builders will be here at ten. I hope you've worked out what you want. If this project is to be up and running by next spring, you'll need to spell it out."

Oh yes, the builders. His project. His plans to breathe new life into Brindle Hall, and into himself. He would turn the decaying Georgian estate into a vibrant business. Josiah Brindle, his entrepreneur forebear, would be proud of him. He had better pull himself together.

His mother, Evelyn Brindle, was in her late fifties. She was slim and vivacious, with dark hair and brown eyes. Sable brown, her husband used to say. She'd passed on these attributes to both her children.

"Freddie is good at his job, Ma. He's done this sort of thing before. He won't let me down."

Freddie Redman was a friend who ran his own building firm. Several months ago, he and Matt had concocted the plans for Brindle Hall during a drunken night in the local pub. Despite its dubious conception, the idea had merit, and Matt had followed it through.

His mother shook her head. "Personally, I think it's too much, too soon. You are supposed to be taking things easy, remember?"

"I need to earn a living, and the estate desperately needs the money. We're sitting on a goldmine here. This house — the entire Brindle estate in fact — is ripe for development."

It was a sore point between them. Evelyn did not want him to return to CID, but she did not want him changing anything on the estate either. As far as she was concerned, things were just fine as they were. But Matt knew very well that they were not. The family was just a hair's breadth away from bankruptcy.

"Not the house, Matthew. I don't want people tramping all over the place."

The same old argument. But his mother wasn't stupid. She must realise they had to do something. For years now, the Brindle estate had been falling into disrepair. His salary as a DI was nowhere near sufficient to cover the upkeep of the grand old house and the land. The family coffers had been at zero for decades. Matt had considered selling part of the land to a developer for housing. He hadn't discussed this with his mother, because he knew exactly what her response would be. This way, apart from the visitors, things could remain very much the same as ever. The bank was prepared to back him, so there was no reason to delay.

He sighed. "We agreed, Ma. We'll open part of the house, the main rooms only, not the private ones. We'll open the gardens, have fishing on the lake, a small petting farm for the kids, tea rooms and a gift shop. We've got all the outbuildings we need. It'll bring in the crowds, but more important, it'll provide the family with a much needed cash injection. There is a lot of interest in the history of this area and what Josiah Brindle did for the people around here. People will come, Ma, and they'll spend money."

"Are you sure about that, Matthew? Do we really need to do this? We're hardly broke."

"We're very close. Cut the injured pride, Ma. We have to face facts. There isn't even enough money to replace the windows in the west gable. We need money to keep this place afloat. The Brindle estate is not what it was. There are no woollen barons like Josiah in the family anymore. Sarah will benefit too. She's on her own with two kids. She can help run the place and earn herself a good wage into the bargain."

"You're sister isn't keen."

"She'll be keen enough when the money starts coming in."

"Where will they put all the cars? I don't want them clogging up the courtyard."

"The lower field will be tarmacked. It'll make a great car park. We'll be able to charge an entrance fee. More money coming in."

Lady Brindle might be a first-class snob, but she did have a practical side. Matt was confident that, given time, she'd see sense. After the 'incident,' as he'd taken to calling it, Matt had been broken, mentally as well as physically. Six months later, despite the limp, his leg had mended reasonably well. The bruises had gone, and the blow to his forehead had left only a very small scar. He had his mother to thank for that. She'd nursed him through it, and he was grateful to her. Evelyn Brindle had dedicated herself to his recovery and had done everything she could to make her son whole again.

But there were parts of Matt Brindle that could not be healed. The mental scars would remain with him for a long time yet. What happened that day had changed his life for ever. It had marked the end of his career in CID, but that was nothing compared to the loss of his sergeant. He had to take part of the blame for that.

He and DS Paula Wright had been searching a derelict cottage up on Marsden Moor. They'd had a tip-off that a local villain had arranged to meet a dealer there, and a large amount of drugs was going to change hands. The tip-off had come from a reliable source and Matt had no reason to be suspicious. But it was a trap, and he and Paula had walked straight into it. Once they were inside, the door was barricaded shut and a hand grenade thrown in through a broken window. Paula Wright was killed instantly, and Matt was badly injured. The memories were bad, sometimes unbearable, but he had to live with them.

"You have costed this thoroughly, Matthew?"

"Yes, and I got Thomas to help me." Thomas had been the family accountant for years. "He thinks it's a great idea. Frankly, Ma, it's either capitalise on what we've got or the National Trust, if they'll take it. How would you feel about that?"

She stuck her nose in the air and tutted. "No. Brindle Hall is your inheritance. Your father would turn in his grave."

"There you are then. Subject closed."

Matt was only in his mid-thirties. Given that his career in the police was over, he needed a project to throw himself into body and soul, something big enough to fill his life. He'd had plenty of time to think it through. He'd formulated the plans for the Brindle estate during the dark hours of recovery.

He closed his dark eyes. He had lived for his work in the police. This thing with the house wasn't simply a way of earning a living, it was a strategy for forgetting, putting his past life behind him. Matt Brindle was hoping that the transformation of the estate, and then running the new enterprise would give him no time to dwell on what might have been. He'd been so ambitious once. He had been looking at making DCI within the next year. After that, who could say? He'd been good at his job, and well liked.

He downed the coffee, and turned on the radio. The reporter trolled through the sport and the weather, but Matt's attention was elsewhere. Then he heard the name 'Alan Fisher,' and he pricked up his ears.

The police were to interview Bella Richards. She wasn't a suspect in Alan's murder, but her child had gone missing. An odd coincidence, if that's what it was. He'd read in the press about what had happened at Victoria Station. When he spoke to Bella at the funeral, she seemed to have precious little information. He hadn't known Alan Fisher well, but he'd seemed a straightforward enough person. It was a mystery why he'd been targeted.

Matt wondered who the SIO was, and if he should have a word. He'd been a policeman for ten years before the incident. He had a good gut instinct, and trusted it. His gut was telling him that the missing child was part of the same crime as the murder of Alan Fisher.

* * *

They'll have done a post-mortem on Fisher by now. They will have seen the mark, the signature, and sent the bullet for analysis, so they will know. They will add Fisher's name to the growing list, and wonder what to do next.

It was the waiting that got to him. He was lonely and itching to start again. He thought about Bella every waking moment. He had been watching her, and knew she would be different. She would not be as demanding as the others. Bella would accept her fate. If she didn't, if she were to fail him, refuse to do what he wanted, then there would be a heavy price to pay. He had the boy, his ace in the hole that would ensure her compliance.

When she disappeared there would be no clues. Not that that was important because no one would even report her missing. He was making sure of that. A couple more loose ends to sort, a short wait for the hullabaloo to calm down, and then he would act.

One of the loose ends was the boy. He might be the ace in the hole, but he needed the police to stop searching for him. He had an idea. He just needed to work on the detail, make sure the plan was perfect, and then he'd be ready.

He picked up the local paper when he went out for his morning walk. No mention of arrests, but it did say that Bella had been questioned, and then released. That was to be expected. What had she told them? Things had happened fast at the railway station, as he had intended they should. All she would remember was the uniform. She had not seen through his disguise, the wig, the prosthetics. If she had, the police would have been banging on his door by now. But he would just make sure.

The second loose end.

He took a photo from his jacket pocket and studied it. It showed a woman in her mid-fifties with curly hair and a wide smile. Bella knew her. She and the boy had visited this woman a number of times. Researching the puzzle that was Bella's life had not been easy. He had no idea if the woman was a relative or a friend, but the man knew enough to know she was a liability. He would have to get rid of her too. She was going to the Costa Blanca on holiday and was expecting a taxi to pick her up and take her to the airport. He would not disappoint.

Chapter 8

"I'm sorry to barge in, but I had to see you. I heard on the news about your son," the man said.

It was Alan's neighbour. Bella had met him at the funeral. "What do you want?" she asked.

He smiled. "To offer my help. You might not remember, but I mentioned that I was a solicitor — Robert Nolan?"

"Why would I need a solicitor?" Bella was puzzled.

"A new senior investigating officer has been put in charge of finding Alan's killer. I spoke to him last night. He's a Detective Superintendent Dyson. I told him, that with your agreement, I would act for you."

Bella didn't understand. "Am I in trouble?"

"No, but you were one of the last people to see Alan. You were with him when he was taken. The police will need to interview you, get your statement. Plus there is your son's disappearance."

She looked at the man. "Surely they can't think that I had anything to do with what happened to Alan, or Olly?" The idea was so far off beam as to be almost funny. But Robert Nolan wasn't laughing.

"I don't know what information the police already have. They may link the two events. In my opinion, you need someone in your corner, Bella."

Robert Nolan reminded her of Alan. A little older perhaps — there were grey flecks around his temples.

"They want to speak to you today," he told her gently. "Since your child is missing, they also want to search this house."

She almost giggled. She was fast becoming hysterical. In the space of a week her world had descended into total madness. "They won't find him here. Why would they think that?"

"It's routine in all missing child cases," he explained. "This morning I will accompany you to the police station where you will answer some questions. While we're away, the house will be searched."

"They won't mess everything up, will they?"

Alison, the policewoman, had been sitting quietly out of the way. Now she said kindly, "I'll make sure they're careful."

* * *

Nolan ushered her into the small interview room and gave her a reassuring smile. "All you have to do is tell them the truth."

"What do they think I know? I can only repeat what I've said already. I told them what happened at the station."

"That's all they need. This is simply procedure. You were there. It's a while now, and you've had time to think. You may have remembered something you didn't think of before."

Bella shook her head. This was torture. Her mind was empty of everything but Oliver. Her son filled her waking thoughts and she dreamt about him at night. She'd taken leave of absence from work. There was no way she could go in, try and pretend things were normal. Not with Oliver missing.

Shortly after Bella and Robert had settled themselves, two detectives entered the room. They introduced themselves as Detective Superintendent Dyson and DC Beckwith. She'd met Beckwith before. They sat on the opposite side of the table. The room was intimidating. The blinds were shut and there was only one small wall light on.

"A few more questions, to get things absolutely clear," Dyson began.

"Is there any news about my son? I'm going out of my mind."

This was a waste of time. They should be out there looking for Olly. Bella glared at them, willing them to argue so that she could let fly at them. "Isn't that where your time would be better spent? He's five, he's alone out there, and you appear to have nothing better to do than pester me!" Her face turned red along with her rising anger. "I don't know what you think I can tell you. I had no part in Alan's death. I loved him. We planned to get married. You are looking in the wrong place!"

Dyson sat back in his chair, apparently unruffled by her outburst. "We never thought you did, Ms Richards. We want your help, that's all. You see, Mr Fisher's death is one in a string of six. So we need you to tell us every single thing you can recall about that day."

He had a nice smile, and he seemed friendly enough. But Bella was gobsmacked. She struggled to take it in. "You're telling me that Alan was the victim of some sort of serial killer? Does that mean he was simply in the wrong place at the wrong time?"

Dyson shook his head. "No, Fisher was targeted. In your original statement you said that the man who came for Alan Fisher knew his name. He knew he had a wife. He also knew where to find you on that station. It was the rush hour. There must have been hundreds of folk hanging about. Therefore he knew what you both looked like. That takes research."

Bella was taken aback. She hadn't given it that much thought. "That means that the policeman who took him away — he killed Alan?"

"At this time we are presuming so."

"And he's done this before?"

"Yes. He always uses the same method to kill his victims, but the way they are taken differs. To date, Ms Richards, you are the only witness who has seen him face to face."

Bella closed her eyes. She saw that this was important, but her nerves were so on edge she couldn't think. She desperately tried to recall every little detail, but her head was a mess. She couldn't see anything beyond Olly, and what might have happened to him.

"I was surprised by his sudden appearance, we both were. To me, he looked like any other policeman." She knew this wasn't helping. "There was nothing odd about his uniform. He had a badge, a radio. He looked the business. When he said why he wanted Alan, told us about his wife, we didn't think to ask questions. Alan went with him and I got the train back to Huddersfield. I was worried when he didn't ring me. Later that night I heard about what had happened on the radio."

Dyson nodded. "He's a cool bugger, our killer, and no mistake. Can you describe him?"

"Not really. All I remember is the uniform. The short sleeved white shirt and the vest thing they wear."

"Accent? Hair colour, anything?"

"He sounded local, northern. I think his hair was fair, but I can't be sure. We were so wrapped up in what he was telling us, I didn't register what he looked like." The superintendent seemed to accept this. "I'm sorry, I don't remember anything that will help. It happened so fast. He was a policeman. I didn't imagine for one moment that he was taking Alan away to kill him!"

She dabbed at her eyes. Bella was annoyed with herself. She'd looked the man full in the face, she knew she had. So why couldn't she remember anything else about him?

"We are looking for your son," Dyson assured her. "We have people out there. He will feature on the local news later today. We would also like you to do an appeal that will go out nationwide."

Bella's nerves began to twitch again. "No! I can't do that," she protested at once. Then she saw their surprise. "I wouldn't be good enough. It wouldn't have the right effect." The three men looked at each other. "Is Alan's death linked to Olly's disappearance?" She tried a change of subject, to get them off her back regarding an appeal.

"The truth is, we don't know. But it's too much of a coincidence, and I'm not happy about it. What's the name of Oliver's father?"

"Gabe Parker," Bella replied.

"Do you think his dad could have taken him?"

"No," Bella replied firmly. "He lives in the north of Scotland, a job on the rigs. you're looking in the wrong place. Gabe enjoys his freedom. He's not interested in being a parent. We don't see or hear very much from him."

Bella looked at Nolan, who hadn't said a word throughout the interview. "What do you think?"

He leaned forward. "I think we have to trust that Superintendent Dyson knows what he is doing."

"You said this man had killed before. Did children go missing with any of the others?"

Dyson shook his head.

"Okay, Ms Richards, we will talk about this again. Thanks for your input."

* * *

Robert Nolan drove her home. Bella sat beside him thinking about the police interview and what Dyson had told her. Once again, her fingers fiddled with the locket.

"Alan gave you that?" Robert broke the silence.

"It was his grandmother's."

"I remember her. She used to go to tea with Alan and Anna every Sunday. A tall, thin woman with short hair and a shorter temper. Anna had no time for her."

Bella shrugged. "I've never met Anna, nor any other member of Alan's family. I've seen photos though. Anna is very attractive. She must hate me."

"She's okay. You needn't worry about her. She won't interfere. Anna is well aware that Alan's money is going elsewhere."

"Have the police spoken to her?"

"Yes, but there isn't much she can tell them. The last time she saw Alan was when he left for the train that morning."

"I still think she must hate me."

"Anna isn't like that. She's a sensible woman. She knew her marriage was over."

* * *

Dyson and DC Beckwith sat on in the interview room after Bella and Nolan had left.

"She asked if kids had gone missing in the other cases, guv," Beckwith said.

"So what? They didn't. I told her the truth."

"You didn't tell her about the dog."

"Would serve no purpose, other than to put the fear of God into her."

"It is similar though."

"It was a bloody dog, son, not a kid!"

"Just saying." Beckwith coughed.

Dyson knew very well what the young DC was getting at. One of the earlier victims, one of those with a green stamp on her arm, looked after a dog all day while its owner went out to work. Shortly before the old woman was killed, the animal disappeared. It turned up a couple of days later, skinned, and hanging from an oak tree in a local wood, with its collar still around its neck. Dyson guessed that the killer presumed the dog had belonged to the woman he murdered.

A uniformed officer entered the room. "Phone call for you, sir. It's Matt Brindle."

Chapter 9

Evelyn Brindle called out to her son. "We've got company. If I didn't know better, I'd say it was Talbot."

"It is Talbot, Ma. I rang him a couple of hours ago and invited him round."

His mother was peering from behind the curtains at the car coming up the drive. He saw the look. She was dying to ask, but was biting back the questions. Matt knew that his mother was terrified of him returning to the force. She didn't like his plans for the house much either, but they were preferable to him going back to CID.

"It's okay. I just want some information, that's all. He won't be here long."

The murder of Alan Fisher intrigued him. He'd known the man, not well or for long, but they'd got on. If he hadn't been killed, Matt was sure he'd have seen him again. He wanted to know what his old team in CID were doing to catch the culprit. He also wanted to know if they were linking the disappearance of Bella's son to the murder.

Superintendent Dyson's car came to a halt outside the front entrance, and Matt went to meet him.

Dyson's thick Yorkshire accent boomed out at him. "DI Brindle. Or are you masquerading as 'Lord Brindle' these days? Quite the country gentleman, aren't you? All you're short of is the hacking jacket and brogues. Seriously though, great place you've got here. I'd forgotten how big it is."

Brindle smiled. "It's not me with the title, that's my mother. My father was made a life peer — services to charity. Now that he is dead, my mother retains the title. She's 'Lady Brindle.' It has nothing to do with me. I inherit nothing but this pile."

"Bloody shame, if you ask me. A title would go well with this old house."

Matt changed the subject. "Good of you to come, Talbot."

"Aye, lad, particularly after you ignored all my emails. Yer wouldn't take my calls, and dismissed my invitation to come in and talk. I tried bloody hard, but you were 'aving none of it."

"Sorry, sir, nothing personal." It had been short-sighted of him. Matt should have known there'd come a day when he'd want something from Talbot. His interest in Fisher's murder and the snatching of Bella's son wouldn't go away. He put it down to the cop in him. That, and having met them both.

"How's your mother? Sick of you yet, is she?"

"Getting there, Talbot. I'm not a good patient. Come in. She'll be pleased to see you. And I really am sorry, I should have got back to you. At least we could have had that conversation." Matt led Dyson up the steps.

"Never mind, lad. We're talking now, and I enjoyed the ride out here. These parts are much more pleasant than Leeds. Your place is in a lovely spot, up here in the hills."

They stood together at the front entrance. From here the gardens swept down to the lake, the well-tended lawn punctuated with colourful flowerbeds. Right in the centre, and drawing the eye, was a large, ornate fountain.

"I'm planning some development. We're going to open part of the house and the grounds to the public."

"Got to admire your ambition. Your mother up for that?" Talbot Dyson sounded dubious.

"It's a necessary evil, I'm afraid. The family, and the estate, need the money."

"So why am I 'ere? What are you after, lad?"

"Information. The team in Huddersfield are currently working on a case I'm interested in, the Alan Fisher murder. Carlisle's got it, I believe."

Dyson grimaced. "Not any more. Things have moved on. The case is mine now. Alan Fisher was killed by an old friend of ours. The 'Mr Apology' killer. Remember him?"

Matt did. Another team had been working on the case when he'd still been active. "Same gun? Shot in the temple? Same mark on his arm?"

Dyson nodded. "A blue stamp this time, the Chinese letters for the word 'sorry,' like with the others."

"I'm interested because I knew Alan. Not well, but well enough to know he was a good sort. He came here to help me with the computer network for the business. I was at his funeral and I met Bella Richards there." Matt smiled.

"We interviewed her this morning. She doesn't remember owt. Her son's gone missing now. I'm praying he doesn't end up like the mutt."

Matt frowned. "So am I, Talbot. But the fact he's been taken has got to be significant."

"We don't know for sure that the two are linked."

"But your gut is telling you they are?" Matt asked.

"Of course they are. You don't think so?"

Matt nodded. "You've been involved with this case since the first murder. I have merely dipped in and out along the way. But there are things about these killings that bother me."

"Careful, lad, you're not one of the team anymore."

"I can't help it. I knew him. I know about the 'apology' killings. I hear and read stuff in the news and to be honest, Talbot, I can't make sense of it."

The two men walked the length of the wide hallway and into a spacious drawing room. The furnishings were opulent, all velvet curtains and sofas. The wallpaper was heavy and elaborate, and was covered with large oil paintings. Dyson stood open-mouthed in front of a portrait above the giant marble fireplace.

"That wasn't there, the last time I was here. Nice-looking girl." He turned to Brindle. "Relative of yours?"

"An ancestor, yes. That's Julianna, wife of Josiah Brindle."

"Didn't believe in covering herself up, did she?" He nodded at the woman's ample décolletage. "A bit chilly up 'ere in Yorkshire for going about like that."

"Julianna was a well-known beauty of her day. She was also an outrageous flirt. That was painted in 1802. We rotate the paintings, that's why you won't have seen it. As we do with a lot of the furniture. We've got loads of stuff stashed in the cellars."

Dyson turned a full circle. "You must have a fortune on these walls. All this antique furniture would fetch a bit too. That cabinet over there," he nodded, "I'm no expert, but I know that's Moorcroft. The room's stuffed to the gills with the stuff. Why don't you raise money by selling some of it?"

"We can't. It's a clause inserted in all the Brindle wills, right from the earliest ones. The collection has to stay put. And it is expected that the incumbent of the day will add to it. So far, I've done very little in that respect."

Dyson stopped in front of another portrait. "Is this the lad himself?"

"Yes, that's Josiah Brindle, the man responsible for the whole thing — the woollen mill and the estate. He was a manufacturer of worsted cloth. He built the mill, this house and the cottages you saw along the lane as you drove up here. They were once millworker's cottages. He employed most of the folk around here. The portrait next to him is his son, Walter. Now he really got the enterprise going. He was one of the investors in the Standedge Tunnel. It made him a lot of money. It carried all sorts of goods and machinery by canal underneath the Pennines, from Manchester to Huddersfield and back again, including our wool. That tunnel really turned a corner for the Brindle family. No longer did they have to cart everything by pack-horse over them hills."

"Quite a history lesson. I bet the punters will lap it up when you get the place up and running." Dyson looked at him. "So what's up, Matt? Why are you really so interested in this case? Is it the connection with Fisher, or is it the job?"

Matt turned to his friend. "Not the job. I'm done with the force. You can see how I'm fixed." He rubbed his leg. "Still gives me trouble. You know how I feel too — after Paula . . ."

"I know how you felt after you were attacked, and I can't say I blame you. But you are a copper at heart. You might try to stay away, bury your head in refurbishing the estate, building your business. But it's not working, is it?"

Matt's old super was right. He had seen right through him. The job was all he'd ever wanted. It still niggled at him, and it wouldn't let up.

"After what happened to Paula, I swore I'd never go back."

"You knew our Paula well enough to appreciate that's not what she'd want. She'd want you back in the job, getting stuck in. If she could see you now, she'd have a right go."

"It's not that simple though, is it? It would be difficult to go back now. There's my mother for a start. She is dead set against it. After all she has done for me, it would be a slap in the face to her. Plus, I submitted my resignation letter to you over three months ago. Even you can't square that one."

"You mean this?" Talbot Dyson's craggy face split in a grin. He took a dog-eared envelope from his pocket and held it aloft. "Sorry, Matt. I hung onto it. Naughty of me I know, but you were too strung out back then. I couldn't let you make such a huge decision in haste."

"So what does it mean? Am I in or out?"

"You're still one of us, Matt. If you want to be, that is. I wrote you off for the duration on a combination of illness and compassionate grounds. A short visit to occupational health just to sign you off, and you're back."

"Talbot! You really are a piece of work!"

Matt smiled. He hadn't felt this good in weeks. He was within a spit of getting his old life back and Talbot was on his side. Matt wanted with his whole being to say yes. Then his smile faded. How could he? His confidence was shot. He was still suffering from panic attacks that came on without warning. The doctor put it down to post-traumatic stress. If he did go back, how would he cope? He didn't want to let anyone down when things got tough.

"The truth is, I need you, Matt." Talbot Dyson took a breath. "I'll do you a deal, make it a little easier. No need to set anything in stone just yet. Give it a try for a week or two, and see how you feel. I'll give you a piece of the Fisher case to get stuck into. After that, we can discuss it some more."

Chapter 10

Bella was staring out of the window at the back garden, her forehead resting against the windowpane. It was early spring so the flower beds were empty. The lawn was waterlogged from all the rain they'd had recently. The entire view was desolate. Which was exactly how she felt.

Alison Wray coughed discreetly from the doorway. "You have a visitor, Bella. He says he's a colleague. Do you want to see him?"

Who is it now? Bella didn't want visitors but still they came. She had not lived here long, just over two years, but people were friendly and by now they'd all heard about what had happened. So they visited. They brought flowers, meals, cake, wine. They were trying to cheer her up, but it was a thankless task. Only Oliver, back home safe and sound, would make her smile again.

She sighed. "Yes, let him in. Are those reporters still outside?"

Alison nodded. "Just a couple of die-hards left. A man from the *Chronicle* and someone from the Leeds papers." She paused. "You do realise that the national media are onto this now? Before long you'll have the daily papers on your case."

That worried Bella. The last thing she wanted was to have her face splashed across the tabloid press.

"The super is still keen on you making an appeal. You could try to reach out to whoever took Olly, ask them to give your boy back."

"I don't feel up to that just now, Alison. Perhaps later." Bella understood why they wanted her to do it, but for the time being, she just couldn't.

Alison smiled kindly. "You have to be guided by Superintendent Dyson. He'll tell you when the time is right."

"I'll let him know."

Alison was about to reply when Joel Dawson stuck his head around the door. "Bella, I'm sorry, I had to come. Find out how you are, and what's happening. Your son . . ."

Joel Dawson was in his mid-forties. He was tall and slight with narrow shoulders. He had cropped brown hair and was obviously growing a beard. It didn't suit him. The dark shadow round his chin made him look older than he was. Still, he was a friendly face, someone Bella trusted. She looked into his familiar eyes and felt as if she were sinking into the pit of despair all over again.

She began to cry. "They say they're doing everything they can, but I don't believe them. They think Olly's disappearance and Alan's murder are connected, but they won't tell me any more than that."

Joel moved a tray of uneaten food from the sofa and sat down, frowning. "You're not eating?"

"I can't. It would choke me." Her voice sounded bleak. Bella drew her long fingers through her hair. She was a mess. When she'd returned from the police station, she'd had a shower and put on her dressing gown. She hadn't even bothered to comb her hair. She wiped at her cheeks. "I'm in no fit state to see people."

"Look, come and sit down. I'm not 'people.' We work together, and we're friends." His voice wavered as he said the last bit. "What happened, Bella? Who took him?"

Bella sat next to him on the sofa and allowed him to put an arm around her. "I have to go out to work. I need the money. It was that damned meeting. I asked a neighbour to pick Olly up. She stopped to talk to someone, and the next minute, Olly was gone. She said she only looked away for a few seconds. My boy must have been terrified."

"They will find him. The police, the public, they will all be looking."

Bella gulped. "He's so little, Joel. And he's not strong. Olly has asthma. He uses an inhaler. He doesn't have it with him. He will be struggling, particularly if he's frightened."

Her tears were falling freely now.

"Have you told the police this?"

"I don't know. I can't remember what I've said."

"You must. They will let the press know. It will be on the news. Whoever is holding Olly will hear and maybe get him a replacement."

That was providing someone was holding Olly, and he wasn't already dead. "Thank you, Joel. I'll tell Alison what you suggested. She'll know what to do."

Bella wanted to smile, to thank him for his concern. But all she really wanted was for him to go. Joel was a considerate man, but irritating. He was the same at work, fetching her endless coffees, picking up her photocopying. When all she wanted was to get on with the job. Was she being too picky? After all Joel was a good sort, dependable and sensible. The type of man she should go for but never did. She always went for the chancers, or the ones that were taken already. It didn't matter now anyway. The only man she'd loved was dead. In her heart of hearts, she knew there'd never be anyone else.

He whispered into her ear. "I'm here if you need me. I know it's hard. I lost Emma a few months ago, remember?"

Bella looked at him. She understood now what he must have gone through when his new bride had been taken from him. "Why is loving someone so painful? I know one thing — I'll never love anyone else. From now on it's just me and Olly. No one else will get a look in. Stuff the lot of them. I can do without the heartbreak."

Joel Dawson said nothing. Bella gave him a wan smile. "I'm no sort of company right now. But I do appreciate your concern, and the visit."

"Everyone at college sends their love," he said. "They're all worried about you. Any news, or if you need any help, let us know."

She grabbed hold of his hand, and looked into his earnest dark eyes. "I can't bear much more of this, Joel. I'm desperate. I just want Olly back, but no one understands. I lost Alan, and that was bad enough — but this! The police questioned me, and I felt like a criminal."

"What have they said about your boy?"

"Nothing. The woman who let you in is from the police. She is staying here, and is supposed to keep me informed. But they aren't doing anything. I feel so helpless. These first few days are important. They should put everything they've got into finding Olly, not waste time and money harassing me."

"You have to keep strong, Bella." He kissed her cheek.

It was a mere peck, but Bella wiped it away. Joel was a good friend, but there was no way she wanted to cross that boundary. She could talk to him because he was a gentle soul. He was like her, he had suffered and he understood. His wife of only two months had died, collapsed on the kitchen floor of their new house. Joel had found her, but not until hours after it had happened, when he got home from work. Emma had been way beyond help by then.

Bella knew he must blame himself. He even said he should have left work earlier. Rang her at lunch. But there had been an open night at college and he'd stayed behind. He'd regret it for the rest of his life.

"I know how hard it is for you losing Alan. I've been there with Emma, but to lose Olly on top . . . you will only survive this if you work hard at keeping it together."

"But I can't, Joel. I'm sinking, going down for the last time, and no one is listening to me." She looked down. "If they don't find Olly, if I can't have him back, then I don't want to go on."

"That's tiredness and stress talking. I don't blame you. I know only too well how that feels. But please, Bella, get professional help, someone to talk to. A counsellor. You have to keep going. Olly could come back to you at any time. You don't know for sure that anything dreadful has happened to him."

She patted his arm. "Joel. You are trying to be kind, but you're not stupid. We've all seen the news. Small children go missing and how many times do they turn up okay?" She shook her head. "He's gone, I know it."

* * *

"Bella, Robert Nolan is here."

"Send him through." She turned to Joel. "Robert is helping me. He's a solicitor, and like you, he knew Alan well. I don't know what I would have done without him."

Of the two men sitting in the room with her, Bella preferred Robert. Although they'd only recently met, she trusted him. Joel was sweet, and a good friend, but there was something needy about him that occasionally creeped her out. She couldn't shake the notion that he was somehow feeding off her grief.

"The police found nothing from the search," Robert began. "They have taken your laptop for analysis. You will get it back, don't worry."

She smiled at him. "Alison made sure they didn't make a mess. They were gone by the time we got back from the police station."

"They've searched your home?" Joel looked surprised.

Robert was sitting facing the two of them. "Just routine. Nothing to get excited about. They are still digging for evidence."

Joel turned to Bella. "Were the police hard on you? What did they ask? What can they think you know?"

"They wanted me to describe the man who took Alan away at the railway station." She gave a small, throaty laugh. "He was dressed as a policeman. The perfect disguise because all I saw was the uniform." She gave a sob. "I looked him right in the face, but I can't bring it to mind, no matter how hard I try."

"You're tired, that's all. You don't know what will come back, given some rest and time," Robert said.

"They want me to do an appeal on TV. Speak to whoever took Olly. But I can't. I'll break down and make a fool of myself. Will you tell them for me, Robert?"

Robert gave her a quizzical look. "It might help, you know, and it is usual in these cases. Are you sure?"

Joel glared at him. "She's said no. Leave it at that. Bella has enough on her plate without the police and you hassling her."

"Perhaps leave it for a day or so, until you're feeling better." Robert smiled at her.

"If I don't get Olly back, I'll never feel better, Robert. You don't have children. I'm hurting from losing Alan, but losing Olly is ripping me apart."

Robert checked his watch. "I have another client to see, but I'll be back, and I'll bring some food. I bet you haven't eaten much, have you?"

Bella shook her head. "I can't eat."

"You'll eat tonight, even if I have to cook you something myself. I seem to remember Alan telling me that Chinese is your favourite?"

Bella nodded resignedly. Why fight? She could already see that Robert was quite a force when in the mood.

Chapter 11

Day 10

For the rest of that day and most of the night, Matt thought about his conversation with Dyson, and the offer he'd made him. He wanted terribly to jump at the chance, dive in and get his life back. The problem was, would his mind and body hold up? And what about the project? Everything was ready for the off. Freddie and his team of builders were all set to start next Monday. Then, of course, there was his mother to consider.

Evelyn Brindle was not happy. "I knew it. The moment I saw him. That man has turned your head. You are not fit to return to the police yet, if ever. You have to face up to that fact, Matthew. What has he promised you? What yarn has he spun you this time?"

"It was me that rang him, Ma. It's a murder case the team are working on. I knew the victim. I was only at his funeral a few days ago. I keep hearing things on the news and I can't just sit by and wonder what's going on. I might make a difference. A small boy has gone missing too, and his disappearance is likely to be linked to it. Plus, I've met his mother, and I want to help."

"You will be run off your feet. You won't have time for anything else. You know what the job does to you." She sighed. "I worry that you won't cope."

"I'll have to get a grip then, won't I? The fact is, I have no choice. I have to investigate. I can't leave it be. Talbot has asked me to give it a couple of weeks. If I can't hack it, then I walk away."

He saw the look his mother gave him. Like him, she very much doubted that that would happen.

"And that's where you are going today? Into the station?"

"Yes, Ma. I'll have a word with Freddie later."

* * *

Matt Brindle stood outside Oliver Richards' primary school. He checked the map on his mobile. Oliver and his mother, Bella, lived a few hundred yards away. He traced the route with his finger. Along the road from the school, past the row of shops and then onto the small housing estate. It was a walk that shouldn't take more than ten minutes.

It was a bitterly cold day, but he hardly felt it. He was too excited at being back in the job. He'd sworn he would never return, that nothing and no one could tempt him. But he'd been wrong. It was in his blood and wouldn't let him be. Matt had made a deal with himself. This case would be the testing ground. If he managed to get through it without falling prey to a panic attack, then he would give his career another shot.

One of the news reports on the local radio had mentioned that Oliver had been seen talking to a man outside the newsagents. Before he checked into the nick, he'd start there.

The road was on a busy through route to Huddersfield. It was unlikely that a small boy could cross it on his own. Beyond the newsagents, where Oliver had been seen talking to the man, was a junction with a side street. That was a likely spot to park a car.

The newsagents was owned and run by Asif Bhatti and his family. Today, his son, Sadiq, was behind the counter.

Matt walked in. A bell jangled at the shop door and Sadiq looked up.

"I'm enquiring about the child abduction that took place outside your shop."

"You police?"

"Yes." Matt showed him his badge. "Detective Inspector Brindle, East Pennine CID."

A lump rose in his throat and he swallowed. He'd never expected to say those words again.

"Do you know Bella Richards and her little boy?"

Sadiq Bhatti nodded. "They come in here most days. Olly gets sweets after school and his comic at the weekend. She's nice, always asks how I am, and he's a good kid. I was on that afternoon. I saw that man talking to the boy. I told the other detective who came asking."

"Would you mind going over it again for me? It might help."

"The lad was staring through the window at the books and comics. I didn't notice much until that bloke came up and joined him. He was pointing stuff out and such. They spoke for a bit, then they walked off."

"Did you see which way they went?"

Sadiq shook his head.

"Do you recall anything about the man? What did he look like?"

"He looked odd. Tall, with a baseball cap on and a ponytail. It was a cold day but he was wearing a T-shirt, and no jumper or jacket."

"Good. You're doing well. I'm impressed that you remember so much."

Sadiq shook his head again. "I know Bella and Olly. It's awful what's happened."

"The man?" Matt urged him.

"It was the tattoos that made me remember him. Huge things up both his arms. I wasn't close enough to see properly but one was a dragon, I'm certain of it."

"Did you tell the police what you've just told me?"

"I told the uniformed officer who took my statement."

"Thank you. That helps a lot."

Matt left the shop and walked the few metres to the junction with the side street. The kidnapper must have had a car, otherwise the pair would have been seen walking along. He looked around — no CCTV and no more shops with nosey staff. This spot would have been perfect.

"It was a Ford, an old red one." The voice came from behind him. "Didn't think much of it until I saw the lad's photo in the paper."

Matt Brindle spun round. The voice belonged to an elderly man on a mobility scooter.

"You've just been asking Sadiq about what happened. I was in the shop, and I overheard. I come this way every day. I take my grandson to school and pick him up in the afternoon. I get the evening paper from the shop. The lad were with some bloke. Big fellow with tattoos all up his arms. He were showing them to the boy. His car were parked there." He nodded towards the side street. "I crossed the road here and trundled on home. I don't know if the lad got in or not."

"Have you spoken to the police?"

"I rang them this morning, but no one's shown up yet."

"Do you know what model of Ford it was?" asked Matt.

"It were an early model 'Ka,' and a 02 plate I think."

Matt thanked the man and returned to his own car. Back to the nick to read through the other statements.

* * *

The CID offices at Huddersfield station were much as Matt remembered them. Only the personnel had changed. In the main office, the desk where Paula Wright had once sat was now occupied by a fresh-faced young man in his early twenties. There were a couple of familiar faces, but most were new. Well, the past was gone. All he could do now was make a try at rebooting his career, as Talbot wanted him to.

Dyson came up behind Matt and slapped him on the back. "You are officially the SIO on the Oliver Richards' disappearance. You can have an occasional loan of Beckwith and one other." He beckoned to a young woman seated by the office window. "I thought our Lily here. DC Lily Haines, this is DI Matt Brindle. He's a good lad, won't give you any bother."

Lily Haines was tiny, no more than five foot tall, with brown wavy hair bobbed on her shoulders. She had an infectious smile that made people warm to her.

"Our Lily is young enough to be streetwise — you know, 'down with the kids,'" Talbot said. "She will be useful."

Lily couldn't have been much older than twenty-five. She was dressed in jeans and a T-shirt and there was a leather jacket hanging over the back of her chair. Paula had liked her jeans too. The day they'd entered that building, she had been dressed much as Lily was now. The memory hurt.

Lily broke the silence. "I've sorted the statements for you."

Matt returned to the present. "Great, Lily. Thanks. Will you put them on my desk?"

Talbot nodded towards a desk by the wall which had a handy bookcase behind it. "Thought you'd like that one. Before we make a start, would you get us a brew, love?" Much to Matt's surprise, Lily trotted off towards a table in the corner that was cluttered with mugs and packets of tea.

"Not very PC that, Talbot. Female staff aren't here to run after the blokes. Things have changed, or haven't you noticed?"

"I carry on as I always have. Sorry if it offends, but during the day this office runs on tea. After dark it's the single malt that keeps things going. And I can't stand that muck from the machine, hence the brew corner over there."

He was a dinosaur, but Dyson got results and he was well liked, so the staff forgave him.

Matt grinned. "The Oliver Richards case — I'd like to look over the incident board for the 'Mr Apology' murders too. Something on there could feed into my case."

"You'll find Carlisle through there. Go easy, he's not having much luck."

Matt went next door. Carlisle was out, but DC Beckwith was hard at it on his computer. "Have you found any connections with the 'apology' killings?"

The DC shook his head. "Random, aren't they?"

This had been said so often that it was now taken for granted, and it bothered Matt. "Even Fisher? That must have taken some planning, surely? He wasn't just spotted and gone for. The killer knew his name. He knew he had a wife. That suggests to me that he'd done some research. Have you discussed that possibility with the others?"

Beckwith gave him a puzzled look. "Still random. All they have in common is the mark." He got up out of his chair. "These three green and these two red. God knows why, because we don't."

"The three green then. Any connection between the victims?"

"Not that we've found."

"The dog thing." Matt nodded at the gruesome photo of the skinned dog.

"We thought it belonged to this one," Beckwith tapped the board. "But it didn't. Apparently she minded it for someone."

"Which someone?"

"Look, I'm sorry, DI Brindle, but I've got a mountain of stuff to do for DI Carlisle. The case file is on my desk. If you want to have a root through it, feel free."

The owner of the dog might be important. Matt had a look at the file, jotted down the address of that particular victim, and left Beckwith to it.

Matt got settled at his desk. There were several statements relating to Oliver's disappearance, but none said anything helpful. He scanned down the list of people Oliver and his mother knew. Neighbours, schoolfriends, teachers. But apart from his parents, there were no other relatives. It rang alarm bells. It seemed strange that there wasn't a single grandparent, auntie, uncle or cousin on that list.

Matt would start with the father. He presumed Gabe Parker had been told, and he was surprised that the man hadn't yet put in an appearance.

"Tea." Lily placed it on the desk and smiled.

"Thanks, Lily, that's good of you. But you don't have to run after me. I'm not the super. Would you check through Records for me? We're looking for a man with tattooed arms and long hair. Anything that involves the local kids, you know the stuff. Also, find out how many people around there own a red Ford Ka on a 02 plate."

* * *

After a frustrating hour of phone calls, it became obvious that Gabe Parker wasn't working on any Scottish oil rig. So why had Bella said he was?

"Lily! We need to have a word with Bella Richards."

"She lives out Meltham way, sir. Want me to drive?"

"Okay. Get anything from Records?"

"Nothing involving a man with the description you gave me. In fact, we've had nothing at all involving men and kids for a while now."

Reassuring, but no help.

* * *

Alison let them in and showed them through to the sitting room. Bella did not seem pleased to see them. She recognised Matt Brindle straight away. "I met you at Alan's funeral. You're a policeman, or you were. What is it you want? I'm sorry if I sound rude but I haven't slept. I was just going for a lie down. I'm really struggling, you know. I can't sleep or eat. All I want is Olly back."

They hadn't been invited to sit down. Matt stood in the doorway and smiled at her. "I'm back doing my old job. As I told you, I knew Alan. I heard what happened to your son on the news, and got curious. I'm now the officer in charge of finding Oliver. If there is anything you want to know, Alison will contact me from now on."

Matt couldn't tell if she was pleased to hear that or not. "I've been going over the statements gathered so far. I've re-interviewed the young man from the newsagents. We now have a description of the man seen talking to your son, and we are following it up." He decided not to tell her about the red car until they knew more. "Have you noticed anyone possibly watching the house recently? Or seen anyone suspicious hanging around when you've been going to and from Oliver's school?"

Bella shook her head. "The only people who have been here lately are Joel, he's a work colleague, and Robert Nolan, the solicitor. He was Alan's neighbour. You will have seen him at the funeral."

"Okay, something else. You told a colleague that Oliver's father works on the rigs in Scotland." She nodded. "I checked, Ms Richards, and he doesn't. None of the companies currently employ anyone with the name Gabe Parker."

Bella ran a hand through her hair. "There must be some mistake. I don't understand what is going on. Perhaps he's left. If that is the case, then I've no idea where he is."

"Has he been in touch?"

She shook her head. "No, we don't talk much, as a rule, only if there is something important to say. The split wasn't pleasant. I do my best to avoid contact with Gabe. He keeps to his side of our bargain, and that suits me fine. I presumed you lot would have told him what's happened. I've heard nothing, so I don't know."

"When did you hear from him last?"

She shrugged. "It must be a month ago. He rang out of the blue and wondered what Olly wanted for his birthday. Odd, he's never done that before."

"Do you have a mobile number?"

"Yes." Bella found the number on her phone and wrote it down for him.

"Does he provide for Oliver? A job on the rigs pays well."

"Yes, he pays an amount each month. There has never been a problem."

"Into your bank?"

Bella nodded.

"If Gabe Parker should hear something on the news and contacts you, we would like to speak to him. Let us know right away."

Bella looked doubtful. "If he has moved on, then he could be gone for a while. A job like his, it can take him anywhere in the world."

Matt and Lily retreated from the doorway. Bella hadn't seemed fazed when he mentioned Parker, and she'd given him the number. Nonetheless, he would check Parker out.

* * *

They were soon back in the car. Lily looked at him. "I have to say, sir, she spoke pretty convincingly about the boy's father. She didn't appear concerned that we wanted to know about him."

But Matt wanted to make sure for himself. He rang the number she'd given him. Nothing. The line was dead, and he doubted the number was valid. Then he rang the nick. He wanted access to Bella's bank account. She had sounded plausible, but his instinct was at it again. He was beginning to suspect that Bella had been telling them a whole tissue of lies. Gabe Parker should have come forward by now. The child's disappearance had front page coverage in the papers. The woman was hiding something, but he couldn't understand why.

He turned to Lily. "Are her phone calls being monitored?"

"I don't know, sir."

"Get that sorted, would you? And a list of her mobile calls."

"What are you thinking, sir?"

"I'm wondering if Bella is being blackmailed."

Chapter 12

The obese woman made her way gingerly down the steep stone staircase, a grunt of pain accompanying every step. She was finding it hard to breathe. The boy's wailing had kept her awake. He had cried for most of the night. Just as well there were no neighbours.

She shouted into the darkness. "Cut the crap, or there'll be nothing to eat!" She kept to the shadows. If the child did leave here alive, she did not want him pointing the finger at her. The boy was bright. He could be trouble later on.

"I want to go home! I want my mum," the boy cried.

The woman muttered under her breath, then called out, "Well, you can't. You've got to stay with me for a bit longer. Your mummy says you have to be a good boy."

The cellar was dark, damp and freezing. It had no windows, no heating. The woman had given him an old duvet for warmth, but the mattress on the bed was thin and damp. She'd fixed the boy's ankle to a hook on the wall with a chain. He could move a metre or so away from the bed, but no more. She didn't want him making a run for it. Overweight and fighting for breath, she'd be no match for a five-year-old if he took to his toes.

"I want my mum! I don't like it here."

His voice was plaintive, interspersed with sobs.

"Cut it out, kid." She felt no sympathy for him, no remorse for what she was doing. If Bella got her boy back, he'd have all the attention he desired. He didn't need any mollycoddling from her. The woman placed a bowl of cereal and water on the floor near the mattress. "Some food for you. And here's a bucket to use as a toilet." She put it down within his reach.

The boy coughed. It sounded harsh, barking.

"What's up with you?"

"I need my inhaler," he wailed.

She had no idea what he was on about. "Shut up and eat. If you're cold, get under that duvet."

"I want to go home. I need my medicine. My mum gives it to me every day."

"What medicine?" The woman inched a little closer, and received a sharp kick on the shins.

"You little sod!" She lashed out with the torch and caught the boy on his arm. He howled in pain and started to cry in earnest.

"Less of that noise. Any more of it, and I'll slit your throat."

Back in the kitchen, she took hold of the phone and flicked through a list of numbers until she found the one for the man who'd brought the lad to her.

"How long? I'm off on holiday at the end of week, so think on. Our Mary will be back by then. If you leave him with her, you're taking a risk. Too soft-hearted, that's 'er trouble. She'll take to the lad, want to help 'im. He needs sorting before then."

She listened. He was telling her to be patient. *Patient!* It was alright for him. He didn't have all the bother, all the crying. The kid was trouble. She'd heard the news. Half of the Yorkshire force was looking for him. It was too risky, and she wanted out.

"End of the week, or you'll get a load of trouble," she threatened.

* * *

Lily raised her eyes from her computer screen. "There is nothing in her bank statements, sir. Her salary from the college gets paid in, and that's it. There's nothing from anyone else. What's more, there's no maintenance payments. So what she said about Parker paying each month was a lie. There are no big payouts either. So the blackmail idea is out the window."

"In that case she's lying to us. But why?" Matt Brindle logged onto his computer and started searching. He wanted to know a lot more about Bella. There had to be a good reason why she'd lie about the child's father.

"Perhaps Gabe Parker has done one. He might not be able to afford the maintenance payments anymore. And she was right about the job he does. He could be anywhere."

"No, she's hiding something, and I want to know what. It could be the reason why her son is missing. Anything on the phone records yet?"

"Her mobile records will be with us this afternoon. She doesn't have a landline."

Matt returned to his research. Bella Richards was turning into a mystery in her own right.

* * *

Two hours later, he was knocking on Dyson's office door.

The super gave him a broad grin. "Settling in? Knew you'd be okay. You couldn't give it up. Policing is in your blood."

"You could be right, sir."

"How are you doing anyway? Any nearer to finding the lad?"

"No, and the case just got a whole lot more complicated. Carlisle is working on the Fisher murder?"

Dyson nodded. "Seemed reasonable, since he was on the other five."

"Do you know if he's looked into Bella's background?"

"You can ask him, but I shouldn't have thought so. She isn't a suspect. What have you found?"

"Between us, Lily and I have checked every set of records we can think of, including births, marriages, and deaths, for both her and the boy. There is nothing. Prior to two years ago, when she moved into that house and started working at the college, neither Bella nor her son has any history. They did not exist, sir."

Talbot frowned. "That can't be right. There must be some mistake, some records missing. She would have given the college references. When she bought that house, they would have done background checks for the mortgage."

"Lily is checking that out now. Meanwhile, I'm going to search the police database."

Dyson shrugged. "I doubt she has a record. It will be some admin cock-up somewhere down the line. Why not ask the woman? Find out where she moved from, see what she has to say."

"I asked her about the boy's father, and she lied about him. We can't find any trace of him anywhere. Her having a record wasn't what I was thinking, sir."

The super logged on to his computer. "Right then, let's have a look, see what we can turn up. I bet that woman hasn't got so much as a parking ticket."

Matt watched Dyson spend the next few minutes searching the police records. "Told you — nothing. Clean as a whistle."

"As I said, a police record wasn't top of my list, sir. But since we can't find any trace of Bella or her son, what about the protected persons programme — you know, the old witness protection?"

Dyson shook his head. "If she's in that, we'll not get anything. We had a case a few months ago in Leeds. The bloke the team wanted to talk to was in the programme. We knew he had vital information, but we were forced to lay off."

Matt's heart sank. If his suspicions were right, that meant information was restricted or not accessible at all, all the way down the line. They could search all they wanted, but they'd find nothing.

"What now, sir? It would help to know a lot more about her. At the very least, who Oliver's father really is. It looks like Gabe Parker is part of the false past that has been created for her."

He watched Dyson wrestle with this. "That's a bit of a leap. Bella Richards is the victim here. Her son's missing. Why would she hold back?"

"So why can't we find her on any of the records, sir?"

"Okay, I'll have a word with the ACC. He might be able to get us something, but I can't promise."

"Impress it upon him, sir. A child's life could be at stake. If we didn't really need the information, we wouldn't be asking."

* * *

When he got back to the office, Lily was still hard at it. "She is a mystery and no mistake. I've been going through the records again, just to make sure. It's as if the woman doesn't exist."

Matt nodded. "She doesn't, Lily. Not as Bella Richards anyway."

"Her mortgage checks out. Her salary was confirmed by the college, and she put down a sizeable deposit. The references she gave the college don't exist. I spoke to personnel, but they refused to comment."

"Told not to comment is more like it."

"There is something. On the statement she gave, we have the boy's date of birth. Of course we have no idea where he was born. But I could find us all the boys registered in the UK with the first name 'Oliver' for that date."

Matt shook his head. "There'll be hundreds of them. Oliver is one of the most popular boys' names. Apart from which, we don't even know if the date of birth is right. It's a thankless task, Lily. We need more to work on."

Chapter 13

Evelyn Brindle was waiting for her son when he returned home that evening.

"How was it?" she said.

"Tiring, Ma, but it felt good being back in the station and getting stuck into a case again."

He'd been wrong to think he could never go back. He'd forgotten the way a case can get to you, and the disappearance of Bella's son had done exactly that. It had drawn him in, and now he was hooked on the job again.

"You surprise me."

She didn't like it, Matt could tell. How to turn things around? He smiled at her. "I now know that I was wrong thinking I could give it up. I was deluding myself. You know how much I loved the job, how much it hurt to have to walk away. But I truly believed I had no choice. I thought that after what happened to Paula, the only thing I could do was quit. I partly blamed myself for what happened, and I was terrified I'd make the same mistake again. I still am to some extent. But that's wrong, Ma. I do need the job and the job needs me."

His mother glared at him. "I can't say I'm pleased. In fact, I'm downright annoyed. But if it makes you happy, Matthew," she shrugged, "I will do my best to cope with the stress. But make no mistake about it, it will wear me out. You are on my mind every second of the day. I couldn't bear it if anything else should happen to you."

Matt knew his mother was a worrier. Now, after the incident, she would be even more anxious.

"I will be very careful, Ma, both with myself and my partner. I know the risks only too well this time around."

"What about the house and your grand plans? If you're working again, that will take up all of your time. It's a huge enterprise, and it needs someone at the helm. If you can't do it, then who do you have in mind?"

His mother had a point. "Sarah," he replied simply. "My sister is more than capable. Like I said, Freddie knows what we want. Sarah just needs to keep him in line, that's all. If anything major comes along, we can sort it together. I don't work for the police twenty-four/seven."

"She was round here today, brought the children. I think she might go for the idea. But you need to put it to her yourself, Matthew. And don't make her feel like second best."

He looked at his mother. "You could help too, you know."

The look she gave him was glacial. "To tell you the truth, Matthew, I don't like the idea of you being back in the force, but I like your plans for the house even less."

He sighed. "We've done that one to death, Ma. The estate needs the money. The project will get the place back on its feet."

Matt had had enough. It was all very well for his mother to criticise his decisions, but she had no alternative to offer. He took a torch and went for his usual evening stroll around the estate. It would take him a good hour, during which time he hoped his mother would mellow.

He walked around the perimeter and then checked the old stables and the outhouses. Freddie had left several pieces of equipment and expensive looking tools lying around, including an industrial-sized cement mixer. He'd need to get a better lock on the door. Once word got round the area about what he was doing, the place would be fair game.

The larger of the old stone outbuildings had been earmarked for the café. The one next to it would be an ice-cream parlour and gift shop. Once Freddie got his team of builders on the job, it would not take long. There was a lake on the edge of the estate, close to the country road that ran through the village. It was fed by a stream, a ribbon of water that trickled down off the hills. It was a lovely spot at this time of year. The spring bulbs were in flower and the ducks were showing off their broods. Matt knew there were carp in there, for his father used to keep it well stocked. The fishing would be good.

Now he had to decide where to place the petting farm. He envisaged starting with a few small animals — rabbits, guinea pigs and the like — for the children to feed.

Oh, why was she so dead set against his plans? He didn't understand why she couldn't see what they were up against. The energy bills alone for a place this size were astronomical. He needed to get her more involved. With Sarah in charge, that became a strong possibility.

* * *

Agnes Harvey walked around her neat bungalow, checking that all the windows and doors were locked. She would be gone for a fortnight and didn't want to invite trouble. Agnes was going to Spain with a friend. They took a holiday together at this time every year. The taxi was arranged for nine p.m. They would pick up her friend Joan on the way, and then it would take them the ten miles or so to Manchester Airport.

Agnes was in her early sixties, slim and with short greying hair. She lived alone and had almost no family. There was a niece, her brother's child. They spoke on the phone from time to time, but not recently, and Agnes couldn't understand why. She knew the young woman was going through some sort of crisis in her life. She'd rung her only yesterday and although tearful, her niece had offered no explanation. Agnes had asked if she could help, even offered to postpone her holiday, but the niece had refused. When she returned, Agnes decided she would get in touch, and find out what was wrong.

She heard the beep of a car horn. The taxi was here. Agnes wheeled her suitcase out to the waiting car and slid onto the back seat while the driver put it in the boot.

"We go via Cheadle to pick up my friend," she reminded him.

He nodded and pulled out of the lane. Soon they were on the dual carriageway, and Agnes settled back into her seat.

It was dark outside and drizzling. They had been driving at speed for fifteen minutes and should have reached Joan's by now. She rubbed at the steamed-up window and squinted out. "I think you must have taken a wrong turn somewhere," she said to the driver.

"Yeah, I just realised," he said. "No worries. I'll take the next right and turn around."

Agnes was surprised. She expected taxi drivers to know their stuff. She used this firm frequently, but she hadn't seen this driver before.

Abruptly he pulled into a layby and turned off the engine.

Her nerves began to jangle. Something was wrong. At this rate they would be late for the plane. "What's going on?"

"The engine is tugging. Give me a moment."

He got out of the car and lifted the bonnet. This wasn't right. She decided she'd better ring Joan, tell her about the delay. But before she could get out her phone, the driver tapped on the window. She rolled it down and looked up at him.

"Sorry about this. Change of plan for you, I'm afraid."

Then she saw the gun. A split second later, she felt it, pushed firm against her temple. For reasons Agnes didn't understand, she was about to die. She screamed and made a grab for him, and her fingers just scraped his wrist. But it was no use. He pulled the trigger.

The woman flopped dead onto the seat, a pool of blood rapidly spreading around her. Shame about the upholstery, he thought, not giving Agnes a second thought. The front seat was virtually wrecked from when he'd shot Fisher. Now the back seat was useless. He'd stash the car for a while and get rid of it when things calmed down.

Chapter 14

Day 11

Lily was already there when Matt came in next morning. "You're in early, sir. Want a cuppa?"

"It's okay, Lily, I can make my own."

"We've got Bella's phone records," she said. "Nothing unusual, but they only go back two years. I can't find a contract in her name before that."

Matt sighed. "Two years. Like everything else in her life."

"There's still nowt on the red Ford. Of course, he could have stuck false plates on it."

"Is the super in yet?"

She shook her head. "Are we going to have another chat with Bella? Maybe if we face her with what we know . . ."

"I'm not sure what we do know. If she is in witness protection and we go storming in, we might jeopardise her new identity. We could be signing her death warrant."

Lily frowned. "Tricky one."

"It's very quiet around here." Matt was looking at the empty desks.

"There was another murder last night. A woman's body was found on a dirt track over Hepworth way."

"I live out there myself," said Matt.

"It's a nice place. Very out in the sticks, with big stone houses."

Matt didn't reply. He didn't like to talk about his own 'big stone house' at work, and especially not the Brindle estate.

"She was killed somewhere else and dumped," said Lily. "Bullet to the temple, and a blue mark on her arm, so she has to be one of the randoms."

"That's two blue marks now. I doubt it's random, though. There must be some connection between this woman and Alan Fisher, otherwise the different coloured marks don't make any sense."

Lily shook her head. "None of it makes any sense if you ask me."

"Do you know where the super has gone?"

"He's gone to take a look at the dump site, and then on to the morgue. The doctor who attended thought the victim might have struck her attacker. Dyson is hoping for some DNA at last."

Matt walked through to the adjoining office. Carlisle was out but DC Beckwith was just coming in. "We've got an identity," he said. "She was an Agnes Harvey and she lived in Cheadle Heath, that's just outside Stockport. CSIs are searching her house right now. Apparently she was off to Spain with a friend. Neighbours saw her get into a taxi last night."

"The taxi firm? Anything on that?" asked Matt.

"She was supposed to pick up a friend on the way to the airport. She says that Agnes Harvey rang the one she always uses, but I doubt it was them that turned up."

That meant the killer had researched the woman's recent history. He knew about the holiday, and which taxi firm she used. "Are you going to check for connections with Fisher?"

Beckwith shrugged. "Yes, but there won't be any."

"You can't know that. Can I suggest that you carry out the task with a more positive attitude?"

Matt spun on his heels and strode back to the office.

Lily looked up when he walked in. "Sir, we've had a phone call. Some of the local high-school kids have been doing a project. They've been doing a survey of the traffic along the Meltham Road at various times of the day."

Matt raised an eyebrow. "That sounds like fun."

"The point is, one or two of them were there when Oliver Richards was taken. One boy was using his mobile phone to video the traffic. His mum has rung in. She says we can go round and take a look."

"Isn't the child in school?" asked Matt.

"No, it's half term, so he's at home."

"In that case, let's go. Where does he live?"

"Up on the tops — Scholes village."

Matt knew where that was. Not too far from his own home, in fact. "I'll drive."

* * *

Luke Standish was fourteen years old, tall for his age and skinny. His face was covered in adolescent pimples that weren't quite acne.

"Thanks for getting in touch," Lily said.

He blushed bright red.

The boy's mother spoke for him. "We heard about the little lad on the news. Luke remembered being on that road the same day."

Matt smiled at Luke. "Let's have a look at what you've got for us."

Luke began searching though the contents of his phone.

"He doesn't remember the man," his mother said. "I don't think it will be much use talking to our Luke, but he's got loads of stuff on that thing."

The boy scrolled through his videos until he found the one he wanted. He handed the phone to Matt. "I think that's 'im."

Matt looked at the footage. Of course, the boy had been focusing on the stream of traffic, but he must have been standing directly across the road from the newsagents. He'd caught Oliver Richards's back view as well as that of the man standing with him.

Matt nodded. "This is good." He watched for a few seconds more. The pair moved off towards the side road where Matt had presumed the man's car was parked. If they could get this enhanced, they might have a reasonable side view of the man. "Do you have anything else?"

"Not for that day. We took that footage then moved on to the junction with the bypass."

"Do you think your friends got anything?"

"The others were logging types of vehicle on their forms. I decided to film them instead. I'll ask, but I doubt they will have anything."

Matt looked at the footage again. "Luke, I'm going to send this to my phone. If you do find anything else, or you remember anything, please let me know." He handed Luke's mother his card.

Back in the car, Matt checked the film. "This is great. We might have a likeness to circulate before the end of the day."

Matt's own mobile rang. It was his mother. She wanted him to return home. Freddie had turned up and was now engaged in a heated discussion with Sarah. According to his mother, they needed Matt to give the final say-so to any change in the original plans. Just what he needed.

He turned to Lily. "A short detour. I'm having some major alterations done at home. Now I've come back to work, I've had to leave my sister in charge. Straight away she wants to change things. My mother reckons they need me to give the final okay."

"You live with your mum and sister?" Lily sounded surprised.

"Just my mother. My sister Sarah lives with her two kids in Hepworth village."

Lily grinned. "Doesn't that cramp your style, having your mum at home?"

What to tell her? Well, she'd see for herself soon enough. "It's not like that. It's a family house. It's big, and I have my own rooms."

"Dark horse, aren't you?"

Matt shrugged. "Not really, I just don't like bringing my personal life to work. The more people know about me, the more they get it wrong. Folk take one look at the house and imagine all sorts of nonsense."

Matt pulled out onto the Sheffield Road. A couple of miles on, he turned up a narrow lane, then climbed a steep hill. He drove on for a further two miles, through the village of Hepworth, until finally, off a side road, they reached the long driveway up to the Hall.

Lily's mouth dropped open. All her amusement at the notion of him living with his mum was gone. "This is where you live? Bloody hell, it's a mansion!"

Matt wished she weren't with him. "I'd appreciate it if you kept my living arrangements to yourself, Lily. I try to keep my private and work life as separate as I can."

"What are you, some sort of landowning lord or something?"

Matt chuckled. "Well, I do own land, yes, but I'm certainly no lord. My ancestors did all the hard work. They earned the money that bought this pile, but it's me that's saddled with its upkeep. Don't be impressed, Lily. Believe me, it's one real hard slog."

He could see from the look on her face that she didn't believe this for a minute. She stared open-mouthed at the lake, then, just as they pulled up in front of the huge Georgian House, one of the peacocks chose that very moment to call loudly and fan its colourful tail feathers at them.

Matt grinned. "That's Hughie. Don't get too close, he's a bad-tempered bugger."

"Can I come in?"

"Yes, of course. Come on, I'll introduce you to my mother."

The minute they stepped through the front door, he heard his mother call out. "Matthew! Freddie has upset Sarah. I'm afraid this isn't going to work."

"Ma, this is Lily, my new work colleague."

His mother looked Lily up and down. She'd disapprove, she always did, but she wouldn't let it show. She'd tell him later when he got home after work.

Evelyn Brindle smiled graciously. "Nice to meet you. Do something, Matthew, before things get ugly!"

"Come on." He nudged Lily. "Let's go and find out what they are up to." Matt led the way back outside, around the side of the house and towards the stone outbuildings. "Freddie is a damn good builder. Sarah is supposed to be looking after the alterations now that I've returned to work. I'm sure whatever changes they've settled on between them will be fine."

When they reached the larger of the two buildings, all was quiet. Matt opened the door and peered in. Freddie and Sarah were deep in conversation, looking at a set of plans.

Sarah looked up. "Mother call you, did she? She doesn't think I'm up to this. At the first sign of me wanting something different," she pointed at the plan, "She runs to you."

"Sorry, sis. She said I was needed."

Matt's sister, Sarah, was tall like him and had the same brown hair, which she wore short. But her face was softer, and she had huge dark brown eyes, fringed with long, black lashes.

"Well, you're not," she said. "We were thrashing out a problem, that's all." She paused, looking at her brother, then at Lily. "You know what this is really about, don't you? She wants you here, where she can keep an eye on you. She's terrified you'll get hurt again. She thinks if you believe I can't manage this, then you'll come running back."

Matt shook his head. "It's a bit late for that. I'll have a word with her later and make her see that everything will be fine. She can't demand that I come all the way up here every time she panics."

"A word? It's our mother you're talking about. She'll listen, she'll nod and then she'll do what she bloody well pleases!"

"What was the discussion about anyway?"

"I put forward the idea of having a link between the café and the gift shop," Freddie told him. "A conservatory. We could site the ice-cream parlour in it, and make the gift shop that much bigger."

"Cost?" Matt asked.

"We'd be saving on repairs to the west end of this building. In effect, we'd demolish that wall. The cost would be a little over budget, but not much."

Matt nodded. "Okay, go ahead. Sarah?"

"Fine with me. Just make sure you and Mum have that conversation. Then I can see to this, and you can get on with solving crimes. But be careful, Matt. Nothing rash."

Chapter 15

When Matt and Lily returned to the station, Dyson and Carlisle were back, and deep in conversation in Dyson's office. Lily took the phone, ready to take it to the tech boys to get the video footage sorted.

"Oliver's lunch bag was found and taken to forensics. Would you find out if they've got anything?" Matt asked her.

Dyson had spotted him and was making a beeline for his desk.

"The search of the latest victim's house has thrown up a bit of a puzzle. This was found on her sideboard." He placed a photograph, in an ornate silver frame, on Matt's desk. "If I'm not mistaken, it's the little lad, Oliver Richards."

Indeed it was. Matt stared at the image of the boy in his school uniform. There it was, the link he'd suspected between the 'Mr Apology' killings and the kidnapping of the boy. Finding the photo also meant that both of the 'blue' victims had known Bella Richards.

Dyson grunted. "This has thrown Carlisle and no mistake."

It hadn't thrown Matt. He'd thought the two cases were linked from the start.

Matt looked at the super. "Bella Richards is at the centre of what happened to Fisher and the woman last night, but why?"

"This could very well have something to do with her past life. We have to consider that if she is on the protection programme, whoever she's hiding from might have found her. This could be an act of revenge."

Matt frowned. "What about our 'Mr Apology?' If your theory is right, sir, how come the pattern is the same as with the others? Whoever she is hiding from can't know the details of the case."

"I don't know, Matt, we can't be sure. It depends on who Bella is running from. There are villains in prison who still have a lot of clout on the outside. People talk. The 'Mr Apology' case has been in the papers, it's been ongoing for a while. Right back at the beginning, that bloody rag published all the details. The reporter tackled one of the uniforms who was still wet behind the ears. The stupid lad gave him the lot."

Matt nodded. "The latest victim, she's called Agnes Harvey, you say?" He jotted the name down. "Given what's happened I will speak to Bella Richards about the woman. If you're right, then she may be connected to Bella's old life. She might be someone Bella could not simply walk away from. We really could do with knowing the truth about Bella Richards's past."

"I've spoken to the ACC. He refuses to help. Reckons if we're right, it would be too dangerous for Bella and her kid. Speaking of which, this came this morning. It was addressed to DI Carlisle, but he's passed it on." He handed Matt an envelope. "It purports to be from Gabe Parker. If it's genuine, then it appears he does exist after all. Parker reckons there's been a spat going on for some time between him and Bella with regard to him having access to the boy. So he took matters into his own hands. He writes that he's got him. Says they're safe and sound, and currently in Stornoway."

"That's the Isle of Lewis. He's taken him far enough away! Has this letter been verified as genuine?"

"We have no way of doing that. We can't find him, remember. Speak to the mother. See if she recognises the handwriting. Get her to talk about her relationship with Parker. I have a bad feeling about this." Dyson shook his head.

Matt sighed wearily. "We need to get this checked out by the police up there straight away. If it checks out, Bella will be pleased that the lad is safe, but I doubt she'll be happy that he's been taken so far away. If Bella does volunteer information about her past, what then, sir?"

"Nothing we can do about that. But she must be made aware of how dangerous it could be for her."

* * *

Matt and Lily pulled up outside Bella's house.

"We'll tell her about the boy. Depending on her reaction, we'll broach the subject of her past. I'm not going to push her, though. She is an intelligent woman. The boy might be with his father, but she will want him back, so we're in with a chance. We'll just have to go carefully. She is going to be upset about that woman's death. Whatever she tells us has to be voluntary, on her own terms."

"So she didn't make Parker up, sir? He isn't simply a name she's pulled out of a hat? There are no maintenance payments, remember."

Matt looked out of the windscreen, lost in thought. "We'll see how she reacts. Gabe Parker may be a false name, but that doesn't mean the boy isn't with his father, or that his father doesn't work on the rigs. It might explain why we can't find him or the false phone number. If she told us the real name of Oliver's father, it would give us a clue as to her real identity."

Lily smiled. "This is turning into a cracking case. I've been in CID for exactly six months, and all the other cases I've worked on have been robberies. Work, but boring, if you get my drift. Up till I started working with you, I was beginning to think it wasn't for me, that I wasn't fitting in. Anything really meaty went elsewhere."

Matt grinned back. "You thought the job wasn't challenging enough for you? Well, this case has put paid to that. And don't worry about not fitting in. I'm still finding my feet too, Lily."

"Surely not, sir. You're an old hand."

"It's not so much the job, it's more my background. People make judgements. They decide things about me based on how and where I live."

"You can hardly blame them, sir. It's a huge house. You must be worth a bob or two."

"I'm not. The house is a constant drain. Once we open it up and hopefully the money starts rolling in, then maybe we'll see."

"I think it's lush. I'd love to live in a place like that. And to think you've given up the chance to run the estate full-time to come back here! Are you happy with that decision, sir?"

Coming out of the blue like that, the question threw Matt for a moment. "I think so. But I didn't expect to get stuck in so deep, so fast. Things have changed since I last worked at the Huddersfield station. The team, for a start. There are new faces, new ideas. This is a complex case. We just have to hope we find all the pieces we need, and put them together correctly."

She nodded. "Like a jigsaw puzzle. That's how I feel, sir. This case has made me feel differently about the job. When I came here, I watched DI Carlisle's team working on the 'Mr Apology' case and I wished I could have a piece of it."

"If we get this right, Lily, there's hope for both of us."

* * *

When Bella opened the front door, all she said was, "Oliver?"

Matt nodded, smiling. "There have been developments, but before we can confirm they're positive, we need your help."

Her face lit up as if it had been switched on. "You've found him! What is it you need to know. When can I see him? Are you sure he's okay?" Alison came and stood beside Bella.

"We'd like to talk to you alone, Bella."

"I'll leave you to it," said Alison. "Got to nip out and do some shopping anyway. Glad he's okay. Good luck." She patted Bella on the shoulder and ran down the front steps.

"Don't keep me in suspense. Where is he? I've been going crazy worrying about him."

"My colleague, DI Carlisle, received a letter this morning allegedly from Oliver's dad, Gabe Parker. It was him who took the boy. He wrote that since he had been denied access, he took matters into his own hands. The pair of them are staying in Stornoway."

Bella's face fell. All her elation vanished, and her eyes, cloudy with disappointment, moved from one detective to the other.

"I'd like you to look at the letter and tell me if you recognise the handwriting as Parker's."

Bella took the slip of paper from Brindle, glanced it then nodded.

"It's okay. We know it's a helluva distance, but the Stornoway police are on it. They will pick Oliver up and he will be brought home to where he belongs."

"Is this some kind of joke?"

Her reaction puzzled Matt. "Absolutely not. Gabe Parker wrote in the letter that the two of you had been arguing about Oliver. So, as a last resort, he snatched the boy and ran. It was very wrong of him, he admitted, but at least we now know that your son is safe."

But Bella still looked unhappy. "Safe? With Gabe? You do not know him like I do."

"Why don't you ring him? He'll confirm what we've told you," Lily suggested.

"I can't." Tears were rolling down her cheeks.

Matt looked at her. "Bella, is it possible that Gabe Parker isn't the real name of Oliver's father?"

The look she threw back was icy. "Of course, that's his name. Do you think I'd lie about something so important?"

Matt was confused. Bella Richards should have been overjoyed. "We did try to contact him ourselves, but the number you gave us for Gabe Parker does not exist. Since he took Oliver, he must have changed his mobile, dumped the old one."

"Yes . . . that'll be it." She spoke in a whisper, her face a picture of abject misery.

Matt didn't understand. She now knew that Oliver was safe. In most cases of child abduction, the outcome was so very different.

"We'll get him back. The Stornoway police will visit the address on the letter. Even if he isn't there, they cannot leave the island. The local police and the ferry company have been alerted. It is only a matter of time before Oliver is returned to you."

"He's not a parcel!" she screamed. "If I thought for one moment he was actually there, I'd go myself." She paused, and then sobbed, "But he isn't."

"How can you know that? We have no reason to disbelieve Gabe Parker. Otherwise why did he write to us at all?"

Bella Richards seemed to be struggling. Matt had the distinct impression that she was on the verge of saying something, but biting back the words.

She took a deep breath. "He'll run. He'll take Oliver and disappear before they get to him. Gabe is clever. He has plenty of contacts on the rigs. He'll have it all worked out. The letter was reassurance, that's all. You forget, I know him of old."

"Then he will be pursued. We won't give up." Matt decided they wouldn't get any further. "Primarily we came to tell you the good news, but I need to ask you something else. Who is this woman?" Matt showed Bella a photo of Agnes Harvey.

Bella took it from him and studied it for a few seconds. "I've no idea. Why? Is she important? Does she have anything to do with Oliver's disappearance?"

She sounded matter of fact. But there was an odd look on her face, and she'd gone very pale. Matt had the feeling that Bella Richards was desperately trying to keep her emotions in check.

"As far as we know, she has nothing to do with Oliver's disappearance. I'm asking because Agnes Harvey was murdered last night — like Alan Fisher." Matt watched Bella Richards closely. She showed no discernible reaction to the news. "Are you sure you don't know her?"

Bella shrugged. "Maybe she knew Alan, or his wife, Anna. Why don't you go and ask her? I've no idea who this woman is."

They were getting nowhere. "I'm asking you about her, Bella, because she had a photograph of your son Oliver on her sideboard. Have you any idea why that would be?"

"Look, DI Brindle. Gabe, Oliver's father, has family. I don't know them, I never did. Perhaps she's related to him. Why don't you go to Scotland, arrest him for what he's done and ask? But I can't help you with this."

Matt looked at her. "We can find no record of you or Oliver prior to two years ago."

She was quick to respond. "So you say. I've moved house. It'll be some admin error, that's all."

"That makes Gabe Parker all the more intriguing. Given he is Oliver's father, he does go back a lot further in your life."

"So — what are you getting at?"

"People you know are dying, Ms Richards. Alan Fisher, and now Agnes Harvey. Perhaps that's why Gabe decided to take Oliver. To keep both himself and the boy safe."

"That's utter nonsense. Alan was murdered by a serial killer. It had nothing to do with me or my past. And I don't know this woman." She thrust the photo at Matt and turned on her heel.

The two detectives followed her into the sitting room. "We know you have secrets, Ms Richards. We suspect that there is a lot about you and your life that you haven't revealed to us. I think it would help us to know more about your background."

She met his gaze. Her eyes were full of unspoken questions. "What do you think I am, some sort of spy?"

"No. I think you are in the witness protection programme."

The silence in the room almost hummed. Bella's expression didn't change. She was good, Matt gave her that. He went on. "And I am becoming increasingly afraid that whoever you are hiding from has something to do with Alan Fisher's death, and Oliver's disappearance."

Bella stared at him, impassive, and appeared to consider this. "Gabe has Oliver. Now that I think about it, I'm sure you are right. He will be safe with Gabe. But you're wrong about my past."

* * *

Bella watched the car pull away from the house. She watched it until it had turned out of the street and onto the main road. She was shaking. Her heart was breaking in two. As soon as the car finally disappeared, she flopped onto the sofa, clutched a cushion and wept.

Someone was playing a cruel game with her. Olly was not with Gabe Parker. How could he be? Gabe Parker did not exist. And now Agnes, her beloved aunt, was dead.

How had that happened? Who knew enough about her and her life to find the very people she was closest to and destroy them? Whoever it was, they had left her with no one. No Alan, no Olly, and no Auntie Agnes to run to when things got hard.

Bella needed help, now more than ever. But not the sort of help DI Brindle could give her. Because of how things were, she could not even bury Agnes. The poor woman had no one else. There would be only neighbours and a few friends at her funeral. Bella would have to skulk around after dark when nobody was about, to leave flowers on her grave.

From the look on that detective's face, he had guessed she was lying to them. But there was no way Bella could admit to having any connection with Agnes, or deny her fictional relationship with the non-existent Gabe Parker. She would pay with her life.

Chapter 16

Day 11

After another haunted, sleepless night, the first thing Bella did that morning was to find out what Alison had planned for the day. Bella needed time alone. She had a phone call to make and it was imperative that no one heard it.

"I'm checking in with my guv'nor this morning," Alison confirmed. "I'll be gone an hour tops. While I'm at the station, I'll ask if there is any news. The police in Stornoway should have an update by now."

Bella didn't reply. She knew very well what that news would be. They wouldn't have found Olly, and no one would recall seeing either of them anywhere. The minute Alison left, Bella went to her greenhouse and took out a rarely used mobile phone from its hiding place. She'd had it since the move to this house, and only ever used it to ring Agnes and one other person. That was James, her contact in the witness protection programme. The man who had set up her new life.

"I need to talk to you," she told him. "Everything has changed. I think he's found me. For the first time in two years, I am really scared. If he knows where I am, the hit could come at any time."

Bella did not think she was overreacting. The man she was hiding from was a violent criminal who hated her.

James was reassuring. "We have no intelligence, no reason to suspect that has happened. We keep very close tabs. We would know if he'd found you."

"Have you not seen the news?" she screamed at him. "My lover and my aunt have both been killed — shot through the head. My son is missing! What more do you need?"

The ensuing silence was punctuated only by Bella's harsh breathing. James had to believe her. She desperately needed his help.

"Calm down, Bella. Okay, I will meet you later today. Take the train into Manchester. Meet me in the local studies room at the Central Library at two. You must not be seen. Given that your son is missing, the police will have you on their radar. Take taxis, and don't walk anywhere. I do not want you picked up on CCTV. We don't want anyone to know that we have met."

Bella said nothing about the police already suspecting the truth. She'd leave that for later. But how to square such a long absence with Alison? She simply wouldn't tell her. It was ten thirty. Bella decided to take the midday train. She rang a taxi firm and arranged to be taken to the train station. She'd have left the house by the time Alison came back.

* * *

The last time Bella had set foot in Victoria Station, she had been with Alan. Overcome with memories of that fateful day, she broke down and wept. People were staring at her, but she didn't care. She dashed through the station and out onto the street. Bella didn't want to look at where she and Alan had been standing then. Being here at all was painful enough.

Another taxi ride later, she was walking towards James. She had not seen or contacted him in two years, but she trusted him completely. He was the only person who knew the whole truth about her life. Two years ago, he had spirited her and Olly out of a situation that could have cost Bella her life, and left Olly with no one. She was eternally grateful for what he'd done.

He was at a table in the far corner of the local studies library, pretending to be engrossed in a book. James was the type of person who blended in. He was in his late thirties, average-looking, never smiled. In his suit, James could be any other business type having a quiet five minutes during the lunch hour. He was difficult to know. He gave nothing away. But that was his job.

Back then, when it had really mattered, he had saved her life. He'd snatched her from danger and made her safe. Up until a week ago, it had all been working perfectly. Then Alan had been killed, Olly taken and now her aunt was dead too. She had to persuade him to help her find out what had gone wrong.

"You weren't followed?"

He was the same old James. No 'hello.' No 'how are you.' He always kept it simple, and entirely professional.

"No. I left while the policewoman was out."

"I wasn't thinking of the police."

Bella felt sick. "Do you know something?"

James gave a little nod. "I've checked out what you told me. It does look like you could be right. I'm afraid that if he has discovered where you are, then you are in grave danger. I'm sorry."

"Don't be sorry for me, James. Just help me get my son back. If this is down to him, I can take comfort from the fact that whatever he might do to me, he will not harm Oliver."

"You think he's had the boy taken?"

Bella nodded. "That is exactly how he would punish me. Plus, he would not want Olly around when he made the hit."

"In that case, someone must be caring for the child. Do you know anyone he might use?"

"He has a sister. Amy. She lives in Wales somewhere."

"Surname?"

"She never married, so it's the same as his."

"I'll make enquiries. We will have to move you on, make you safe again."

Bella swallowed. "No, James. I don't want that again. I've done it once and that was enough."

"What do you want then? Why am I here?"

"I want to see him." She saw the look on his face. He didn't like this at all. "I want to ask him straight out what he's done with our son."

He shook his head. "That is out of the question."

"I don't see why. It would be a simple prison visit."

"No it wouldn't, and you know why. He wants you dead. You gave evidence against him, and he went down for multiple murders. He isn't getting out, Bella, and he blames you for that."

"I want to ask him about Oliver, face to face," she said again. "He can't harm me if he's in prison."

"You cannot take the risk. Your theory that he is behind the killings might not be correct. They may have nothing to do with him. What do you do then, Bella?"

"Of course, he's behind it," she scoffed. "Who else would want all those closest to me dead?"

"Even so, you will give him information he will use, and you won't even realise it. He is a clever man, Bella."

"I'm not arguing, James. Organise this for me, or I'll do it myself."

He shook his head. "It won't be easy. You are on the programme."

Her laugh was almost a giggle. "My cover is shot anyway. What have I got to lose?"

"I'll contact you. Keep the phone handy."

Chapter 17

Carlisle walked over to Matt's desk. He looked angry. "Alison Wray has been on the phone. The Richards woman has done one. What did you say to her?"

Matt wasn't going to discuss that with Carlisle. "Is she sure?"

"Yes, and she left her mobile behind, which she never usually does."

Matt decided to return to Bella's house, to ask if any of the neighbours had seen or heard anything.

Lily was puzzled when he told her. "Why would she do a runner, sir? Given that her son has been located and about to be returned to her? She's been desperate for news all week. Leaving her phone behind sounds dodgy too. The thing lives in her hand."

"We'll find her," said Matt.

"What if this is down to the man she's hiding from? What if he's taken her?"

Matt held up a hand. "Let's not get ahead of ourselves. There may be a simpler explanation."

"What makes you think anyone will have seen where Bella went?"

"Because it's that kind of street. All her neighbours know what has happened. Bella has hardly left the house in the last week. She'll have been spotted, take my word for it."

* * *

Within half an hour, Matt and Lily were knocking on doors all along Bella's street. They soon learned that she'd left the house alone and taken a taxi. Lily went back to the car and started ringing round the local firms.

"Yorky Cabs, sir!" she called out to Matt, who was still at it. "She was taken to the railway station in Huddersfield. She wanted to be there by one. The driver reckons she was getting the Manchester train."

Matt got back in the car. "She could have been going anywhere. We'll go back to the police station and see if we can pick her up on CCTV."

"Do you think she went to see someone?"

"Well, I don't think she went for a browse round the shops, Lily. When we get back, check her phone records, see if she rang anyone or received a call before she went out."

Back at the station, Lily contacted security at Victoria Station, who emailed the footage of the platform where the Huddersfield train pulled in. The film covered a period of two hours. Matt fast-forwarded to just before two and they watched.

The train pulled in and around two dozen people got off. One of the last to alight was Bella Richards. She appeared to be in a daze, with no makeup on her face and messy hair. She was carrying a shoulder bag and had a mobile phone in her hand.

Matt pointed. "She has a second phone. We must ask her about that."

"What now, sir?"

"Well, we could do with knowing where she's going."

"I could try and get hold of the street footage," Lily suggested.

Just then, Matt's phone rang. It was Alison Wray.

"Bella is back home. She arrived a few minutes ago looking shattered, and went straight up to bed without saying a word."

"Okay. Don't push her, but make sure you know exactly where she's going next time, she can't just wander off on her own. It's getting late. I'll speak to her in the morning."

Lily looked at him. "She's still in one piece, then?"

"Yes, Lily. We will get to the bottom of this, but we'll give Bella time to think things over. My guess is that she went to meet someone — secretly. If we're going with her being in witness protection, that someone could have been her contact. And if that's so, she won't tell us anything anyway."

"We've had the forensics back on the boy's bag by the way." Lily accessed the report. "Nothing much. A mishmash of fingerprints, some of which belong to a child — presumably the boy — and Bella's."

"The kidnapper will have worn gloves when he ditched it."

Lily was reading through a second report. "No one noticed anything odd on the moorland roads either. He must have known how quiet they are, that'll be why he used them."

"Not daft, our killer, is he?"

* * *

Bella had a lot to think about. What she really needed was someone to talk to. Agnes had been the only person to know her situation apart from James. Bella lay in bed, considering whether to confide in someone else. But who? Not one of her colleagues — word would spread around college like wildfire. Nolan perhaps? He was a solicitor. He had said he wanted to help. But could she tell him the truth about her past?

"Are you okay, Bella?"

It was Alison, bringing her some tea. Bella looked up at her and smiled. "Getting there. Any news? Have the Stornoway police checked that address?" Bella asked simply because it was expected of her. She knew very well that Olly wasn't there.

Alison shook her head. "We've heard nothing yet. Where did you go today? You had everyone terribly worried. My guv'nor was livid."

"I'm sorry. I didn't intend to get you into trouble. I had to get out. I felt trapped in these four walls. Stupid of me, I know."

"You were gone a while."

"I took the train into Manchester. I wanted to see the station again. It was the last place I saw Alan alive and spoke to him. I hung around for a bit and then I got the train home."

Bella could see from Alison's face that she didn't believe her. Well, she didn't care. The police could do nothing for her, no matter how hard they tried. There was only one course of action — to fix this herself. With luck, James would arrange the visit within a matter of days. Then she would know.

Chapter 18

Day 13

"You will do exactly as I tell you, Bella," James said. "I will accompany you to the waiting room but no further. You will meet your ex-husband in a private room. There will be the two of you and a warden present. Your conversation will be recorded. Do not answer his questions. The whole point of this is that he answers yours. You must not give him anything he can use to find you." He paused for a moment. "There must be no physical contact either."

Bella nodded. She'd do anything. She just wanted him to talk to her, tell her what had happened to Oliver. At the same time she was nervous. Bella had last seen him over two years ago, in court, after the judge had passed sentence. The look he'd given her then was venomous. He had been led away cursing her, screaming death threats and obscenities. He hated her with a passion.

But he loved his son.

"Take all the time you need. I've sorted things with the FLO and the investigating officers. Good luck." James pushed her forward gently.

Bella was terrified. She was a very different person now from the one he would remember. But what about him? She'd loved him once, in another life. Back then she'd known nothing about the world he inhabited. He had been the man of her dreams. How could she have been so gullible? How could she not have seen him for what he really was, a brutal killer who showed no mercy? How could she have married one of Manchester's most infamous villains, and not have known?

In the months that followed his arrest, Bella believed he must have brainwashed her. But the truth was much simpler. Bella wouldn't listen. People had tried to tell her, Agnes in particular, but Bella had been so besotted that she'd ignored them all.

She walked slowly into the room. He looked relaxed, harmless, nothing like the hype at all. Just a tall, thin man who had dimples in his cheeks when he smiled. Still in his mid-forties, he should have had everything to live for. He certainly didn't look like a villain. There were no scars, no tattoos, only a big smile on his face when he looked up and saw her.

Bella felt the tears well in her eyes. His dark hair was cut very short and he looked pale. He'd always been so proud of his tan and his designer clothes. Now he was dressed in a prison overall, looking just like any other bloke. Ordinary. But he wasn't just any other bloke.

"How you doing, doll? You look good. You smell good too."

Bella inched forward. She began to shake. Perhaps James was right, and she should never have done this. "Ronnie, I . . . I want to talk to you."

Ronnie Chalker lifted his slight shoulders and shrugged. "Talk away, babe. It's been a while. We've a lot to catch up on. I was hoping you'd come and visit sooner. I've missed you."

He sounded so matter of fact, so reasonable. But Ronnie Chalker wasn't reasonable. He would share a joke with his enemy, then shoot him in the head while they laughed together. He was hard, calculating, and very dangerous.

"Why so nice? You hate me. You must hate me after what . . . what I did."

"Time passes, things change. I've changed." He gave another shrug. "I had an accident. I fell down the stairs and got a bang on the head. It put me in hospital for ages. It made me different."

No one had told her that. "Are you alright now?"

"They say so. I've had scans and tests. The doctor says there was some brain damage. The back of my skull was broken. It's left a scar on my brain. The upshot is, I'm not the same man. Those awful moods, all that anger I used to have, it's all gone. I've got gaps in my memory too."

Dare she believe him? Was this part of some elaborate plan? Two years had passed since the court case. He'd certainly hated her then. He'd wanted to kill her. Bella was sure that not enough time had passed for him to have changed his mind.

"How did you fall? Was it an accident?"

"I don't remember. The screws say it was. Never mind that. What have you been up to, Izzie? Tell me about Olly. How is my little man?"

Izzie. It seemed like a lifetime since anyone had called her that. When she'd gone into witness protection she'd had to choose a different name. She'd chosen Bella because it was a derivative of Isabelle, and Richards was her mother's maiden name. Ronnie, of course, knew none of this.

Bella searched his face, stared into his eyes. Was he telling the truth about the accident? He did seem different, much more placid. But she just couldn't be sure.

"You tell *me* how Oliver is, Ronnie. You're the one who has had him taken."

He stared at her for a few moments and then laughed. "You're crediting me with something there, babe. Had our Olly taken, have I? Now there's an idea!" His expression changed. A frown clouded his face, and his dark eyes shrank to pinpricks. "What you saying, doll? What's happened?" The edge was back, the sharp, staccato tone that Bella remembered so well.

"Olly was taken. He's been gone a week and the police can't find him. People close to me have been murdered, Agnes has." She continued to stare into his eyes. "They were shot in the head. In the temple, Ronnie! It was your favoured method of killing, so I'm told."

He laughed again, shaking his head. "You think I've had people killed? You think I've had my own son kidnapped? In case you hadn't noticed, babe, I'm banged up. I'm done with all that. No choice, have I?"

"I don't believe you, Ronnie. I think you had Alan Fisher killed and Agnes too. I also think you've had Olly taken from me as punishment for what I did to you. Who is looking after him? He needs care. He has asthma, and hasn't got his inhaler."

Ronnie Chalker leaned forward suddenly. The warden made a move to interfere but Ronnie waved him away.

"Be very careful, Izzie. Accident or not, I'm still capable of losing it, particularly if I'm pushed. I won't let you stitch me up again, so don't even try."

"This is no joke, Ronnie. Olly has been taken. I came here today to find out if it's down to you."

He spoke slowly and deliberately. "I have no idea who Alan Fisher is. I knew Agnes, of course, and I'm sorry she's dead. As for our son, I'm not stupid, Izzie. His place is with you. I've spent days, weeks, trying to come to terms with what you did to me. In the early days, if I could have got hold of you I would have throttled the life out of you with my bare hands. But since the accident, I've changed."

Was this the truth? Bella couldn't tell. His eyes told her nothing. She couldn't read him. He was always very good at keeping his real thoughts to himself.

Her voice faltered. "You're not lying about Olly? You swear you haven't taken him?"

"I owe you nothing, Izzie. It gladdens my heart to see you suffering. I don't want to ease your pain, not in the least. But I had nothing to do with Olly's disappearance, I promise you. You need to find him."

"What are you saying?"

"I didn't have him taken. But I will promise you this. If anyone on the outside hurts my boy, banged up or not, I'll have his head."

"Has Amy got him, your sister? She would help you if you asked."

"Amy disowned me. I don't even know where she's living these days."

Bella almost reached out to touch him. She withdrew her hand. "I need to know, Ronnie. This isn't about me, it's about Olly. He gets ill, he needs his medication. If you know anything, you have to tell me."

Ronnie Chalker smirked. "Make no mistake about it. I hate what's happening to Olly, babe. He's my only child. I'm banged up in here and powerless to do anything about it. How do you think that makes me feel? But on the plus side, loving all the worry it's causing you. It's playing havoc with your looks."

"This is not about me!" she shrieked. "I just want Olly safe! Surely you want that too? You're his father, for God's sake!"

He slapped his hands down on his knees. "Okay, fun and games over. Not me this time. No way would I harm my own son. You know how I idolised that child."

"So what's happened to him?" Bella said. All the stomach-churning panic rushed back. Bella had been so certain that Ronnie had had Olly taken to punish her. That thought alone had kept her sane. If that was the case, she knew the boy would be looked after. Ronnie loved his son. But now he was telling her he had nothing to do with it.

He ran a hand over his barbered hair. "The police will have to try harder to find him. It's up to you to crack the whip, babe. Someone must know where he is. Look around you, Izzie. It will be some idiot in your circle of friends who has done this, or someone you work with. Make the police work it out." He leaned towards her slightly. "Get him back Izzie," he hissed at her. "Because if anything happens to Olly, it won't be pretty. I'll have the bastard found, and you'll suffer too for letting this happen." He leaned back again. The smile was back. "You know what I'm saying, babe? You understand how things are?"

Bella understood only too well. Ronnie had nothing to do with Olly's disappearance, but worse than that, he blamed her. The realisation that Olly might be lost to her forever tore at her heart. Her tears spilled out, and she could do nothing to stop them.

Chapter 19

Bella returned home shattered. The prison was a few miles outside York, a car journey lasting an hour or so. James had dropped her off in Huddersfield centre and she'd caught the local bus to Meltham. When Bella walked in, Alison did not ask prying questions, just if she'd had a good day. Bella had made up an excuse that she had to have some time on her own, and had spent the day window shopping in Huddersfield. Alison was fine with that, as long as she checked in every two hours by text.

"Any news?" The same old words, and the same old answer — a shake of the head. "Tell that Detective Brindle that I want to know what he is doing to find my son. It is taking far too long." Bella went upstairs for a lie down.

She had a lot to think about. On the journey back, she'd asked James about Ronnie's accident. She wanted him to confirm the details. If Ronnie had told her the truth, it was possible that he was no longer the threat he'd once been. The hard edge was still there, but he seemed subdued, less angry. Once she'd impressed upon him that Olly was in real danger, he'd urged her to get help.

But now Bella had to face the awful truth. Someone else out there was hell-bent on ruining her life. Someone who hated her even more than Ronnie was systematically eliminating everyone she held dear.

Alison brought her a cup of tea. "Joel Dawson came round while you were out. You'd only been gone a few minutes when he was at the door. An odd man, that. Wanted to know exactly where you were, and got proper shirty when I couldn't tell him."

"It's just his way. Joel gets anxious. Don't worry, I'll ring him later."

Joel was a friend, one of the few she had left. He understood, and Bella didn't want him being upset. She was going to need people like him to keep her sane. Bella was facing the hardest time of her life.

* * *

She slept soundly for a couple of hours, until Alison woke her. "DI Brindle is here. He wants a word."

Bella dressed hurriedly and went downstairs. She wanted information. If she believed what Ronnie had told her — and she thought she did — it meant that she had no choice but to rely on the police. The big question was, how much should she tell them?

She made her decision. "I have to tell you something. Oliver is not in Stornoway. He was not spirited away by Gabe Parker, I can assure you of that."

Lily looked at her. "How can you be so sure? Has Mr Parker been in touch?"

"There is no Gabe Parker."

DI Brindle cleared his throat. Bella knew he had suspected as much.

"Would you like to explain, Ms Richards? This is vital information. We needed to know this from the start."

"I moved here two years ago. Oliver had no dad. I didn't want folk gossiping about us, so I made one up. I told everyone that Gabe was working miles away on the rigs in Scotland. That way no one would expect to see him around."

Brindle was silent for a moment or two. "Why didn't you tell us that sooner?"

"I didn't think it was important. I never expected you to get that letter."

"Given what you've just told us, do you have any idea who sent it?"

Bella lowered her head. "No, and that's the truth. I made no secret of Gabe Parker. My work colleagues, the people who live around here, all of Olly's friends knew the name, and where he was. Anyone could have written that letter."

Brindle looked hard at her. "I cannot stress enough how important it is that you tell us everything, Ms Richards. If Gabe Parker is a fiction, what about the rest of your past? Do you feel any more inclined to tell us where you were and what you were doing up until two years ago? It might help us with the investigation."

"This again! Now that I've levelled with you, your time would be better spent looking for Olly. Remember him? The missing five-year-old boy? He's out there somewhere, he's alone and he needs me. I'm going out of my mind with worry." Bella began to cry.

"We have one or two leads. Have a look at this photo." The DI handed her the photo of the man who'd been seen with Oliver outside the newsagents.

"I don't know him. Who is he?"

"Is that the policeman who took Alan Fisher from Victoria Station?"

Bella looked at the image again. It was taken from the side, so there was no clear view of his face. "No, it's nothing like him. This man has long hair, and look at those arms. The policeman had short hair. He was wearing a short sleeved shirt too. There were certainly no tattoos on his arms."

"You don't know him from anywhere else?"

Bella shook her head.

"Ms Richards, two days ago and again today, you went off somewhere on your own. Where did you go?"

She looked away. "That is none of your business."

"We also know that you have a second mobile phone," he said.

"What if I do?"

"You took the second phone into Manchester with you the day before yesterday. You left your usual phone here in the house. We saw the second one on CCTV footage of you at Victoria Station. Who do you use it to contact?"

"As I said, it's none of your business. Lots of people have more than one phone." She tilted her head, her tears gone. "If you spent as much time looking for Olly as you do spying on me, you might have found him by now."

"Do you believe that Oliver's disappearance has anything to do with your life before you moved to Meltham?"

Bella shook her head. "No, I don't."

"How can you be sure?"

"I am, and that's all I'm prepared to say."

* * *

Back in the car, Matt looked at the photo of the man again. "She really didn't know him," he said to Lily. "I could see that much in her face."

"She seemed positive that Oliver's kidnapping had nothing to do with her old life."

"I'm not sure I believe her on that one."

"So what's going on, sir? What are we missing?"

Matt frowned. "I think she's lying. Trying to protect herself. Or perhaps we're looking in the wrong place, at the wrong things. We're looking at her past because the super reckons we should. To be fair, it was always a possibility, given that we believe she's in witness protection. I think Bella was thinking along the same lines.

But something has changed. Bella went out this morning. Try as I might, I can't find out where she went."

"But it's got you thinking, hasn't it, sir?"

"It's a hunch, nothing more, but think about it, Lily. If you thought someone you were being protected from had taken your child, what would you do?"

"That would depend. If that person was someone I'd been close to once, and if it was possible, I would go and ask him."

"Exactly. I think Bella Richards went on a prison visit earlier today. The arrangements were made quickly, and maybe the visit was outside normal visiting times. If we knew which prison, they will have a record of it."

Lily smiled. "I could make some discreet enquiries, sir. She was there and back in a day. So it's reasonably local — Strangeways or York perhaps."

Matt Brindle was warming to Lily. She was bright and keen to do well. He'd no idea how long they might continue to work together. He was still on probation, as it were, and Lily was sent wherever she was needed. He'd worked with DS Paula Wright for years. By the end of their time together, they would invariably come up with the same theories, share the same hunches. Matt didn't know if he'd ever find that sort of relationship with another detective, but Lily was doing alright.

Chapter 20

Bella rang Robert and asked if he would see her. He came straight away. "I'm worried that the police are not doing enough."

"I know it's been several days now, but they are doing everything they can," he reassured her. "It's very difficult. They have nothing to go on."

"You don't understand. They know something about me, and that has coloured their view of the case. The police believe that someone from my past may have taken Olly in order to punish me. Before today, I thought so too. To be honest, that's what kept me going. I knew that the person I had in mind would never hurt Olly. But now I know they had nothing to do with his disappearance."

Robert looked confused.

"I have a past," she explained. "It's not something I can discuss with anybody, not even you. If I did, it could put both me and Olly in danger."

"I'm sorry, Bella, but you'll have to explain a little further. I'm your solicitor, you can trust me. Anything you say is in the strictest confidence."

Bella was torn. She wanted to tell him. She needed someone to talk to. She wanted to discuss what Ronnie had said to her. Robert was the only person left that she could confide in.

She sighed. "I'm in the witness protection programme. You realise what that means?"

He was staring at her, his face a blank. "It means you are not who you say you are. That your current life is a sham."

Harsh, but nonetheless true. "If there had been any other way, Robert, do you think I wouldn't have taken it?" He didn't answer. "I did think that the man they are protecting me from had taken Olly, that he'd found me and was taking his revenge. Not against Olly, against me. It is exactly his style."

"How do you know that isn't true?"

"The man was once my husband, Olly's father. I know he loves his son and that he would never hurt him. I visited him in prison and asked him." She paused. Robert looked shocked. "He did not take Olly, so I am back to square one."

"Who is he, this man?"

"I can't tell you."

"You have to be absolutely sure that he is not involved."

"He isn't," she insisted.

"Okay, I'll speak to the police, push them into doing more."

* * *

It was getting late but there was still work to do. Matt needed to formulate a plan for moving forward with the case. He and Lily returned to the station and checked what had come in. If they were not looking at Bella's past for an answer, where were they going to look?

"There was DNA under Agnes Harvey's nails." Lily was looking at the results on her computer screen. "But no match I'm afraid."
Matt sat at his desk. If what Bella had told them was true, they had been seriously side-tracked by their belief that she was in witness protection. But if she wasn't, then who was destroying her life? She was an ordinary woman, living a normal life. Who could she have upset so much that they would do this to her? "This has to be retribution," he decided. "Perhaps a rival villain with a grudge, getting even."

Lily shrugged. "It would be helpful if we knew who her villain boyfriend, husband or whatever is."

"The other five 'Mr Apology' murders — do we have the case files?"

Lily peered through the window into his office. "They will be with DI Carlisle. He's out. He'll have left them on his desk."

Matt went to get them. It might be Carlisle's case, but Oliver Richards's disappearance was part of it. He spent the next hour or so poring over the files.

Finally he closed the last file. "There's nothing much. As far as I can see, the killer hasn't put a foot wrong — except for the dog. The killer thought the dog belonged to Marjory Bentley, one of the green stamp victims. But it didn't, she merely looked after it. Do we know who for?"

Lily looked up. "It should be in the file, sir. Whoever did own the poor thing must have been told."

But it wasn't in the file. In fact there was no mention of who the dog belonged to.

"Mind you, the dog wasn't found straight away. It turned up after a few days." Lily shuddered. "Bit too gruesome for me, a skinned dog."

"Are we sure it was the right dog?"

"The collar had a tag on it, sir. There were two addresses — the owner's and that of Marjory Bentley."

Matt decided to have a look at it. "Finish off and go home, Lily."

"What about you, sir?"

"I'm going to have a look at the evidence for this case, then I'll call it a day."

"You're after that dog tag, aren't you, sir?"

"That's where I intend to start, Lily."

* * *

Bella was tired. It had been a long day. A knock on the door so late in the evening made her heart sink.

"Joel!" She was surprised to see her friend and colleague standing on the step.

"I've been really worried about you, Bella. You must be going out of your mind. I've heard conflicting reports on the news. This morning they were saying the police knew where Oliver was, and now they're saying he's still missing. Do you know what's going on?"

Bella let him in and he followed her down the hallway into the sitting room.

"Everyone at college sends their best."

She shook her head. "I'm tired, Joel. I'm not up to conversation, not tonight."

"I saw that solicitor leave. He was here a while. Has he been pestering you?"

Bella gave him a quizzical look. Had Joel been watching her? "Robert is a great help. He's acting for me, so we have things to discuss. He isn't charging me either. Have you been spying on me?"

His face fell. "I worry that whoever took Oliver might come back and try to harm you. If I'm close, keeping an eye out, at least I'll know you're safe. If anything does go wrong, I'll be able to tell the police straight away."

Bella gave a little shiver. "That's not necessary. Besides, I don't like to think of you hanging around out there. I know you mean well, but the idea of someone spying on me freaks me out. You have to understand. Things are bad enough as they are."

It wasn't just her imagination. On one level Joel was fine, but if you delved below the surface he was creepy.

"You got into a strange man's car today. He met you off the bus in Meltham. I was worried so I tailed you. Why did you go to that prison? Do you know someone there?"

He had followed her! This was far worse than creepy. This bordered on obsession. "You have no right to follow me, Joel! You have to stop it. You must believe me when I tell you that I'm fine."

"So who was he?"

"Just someone I know. A friend who is helping me."

"Like Nolan?"

"Yes, but in a different way. Look, Joel, this has to stop." Bella knew he meant well, but Joel Dawson could become a liability. If he found out about her old life and told someone . . . "I have secrets. I'm not prepared to talk about them, so don't ask, and don't gossip about me either. That man you saw me with is part of a life I've walked away from."

"I won't breathe a word. You can trust me, Bella. I've noticed that you don't talk about the past."

"That's deliberate. And I don't want to talk about it now. It's safer all round."

"After Emma, I hated being alone. I thought you might feel the same, want some company. Need a friend to talk things over with."

Bella sighed. "There is a policewoman staying with me. And I've got Robert on speed-dial." His face fell. "Go home, Joel. Stop worrying about me. I need to get some rest."

"How does he help you? He's a stranger. Robert doesn't know you like I do. Why won't you let me in, Bella? I can help, bring you some comfort."

Bella looked at him. His face wore that earnest expression she knew so well. "Olly's disappearance is complicated. There are things about me that no one knows about. I've told Robert a little, but I can't reveal any more. It might put me in danger."

"I can't begin to understand what you're talking about. I won't let anything happen to you." He made a grab for her arm. "I want to help. I need to help, to be near you. You have to let someone in, Bella, so why not me?"

"You shouldn't get involved, Joel. I'm trouble. I have a past. I used to know some bad people, one man in particular. If he finds out where I am, he'll have me killed."

Joel looked shocked. "Someone is looking for you, that's it. You have run away from something awful, and hidden yourself in this backwater."

"Something like that. Now let it drop, please."

Chapter 21

His information about Bella's life was almost complete. But until he was ready, it was imperative that no one came looking. The obvious contenders had been dealt with. But the police were tenacious, particularly that Brindle bloke. And the boy was an irritation he could do without. His face was plastered across every newspaper in the country, and he was hardly ever off the TV news. He would have to be careful. One solution to the problem of the boy was to get rid, so that he would never be found. If need be, Cora would help him with that. The problem of Brindle, however, would need some thought.

Still, he was certain that Bella would soon be with him. A little while longer, once the hullabaloo over the boy's disappearance had quietened down, and then he would take her. But before he could even contemplate that, he would have to deal with Bella's predecessor.

The young woman who'd been his for nearly eighteen months was stretched out naked and still on a bench in the cellar. In life she had been a beauty. However, in death she was fast turning rancid, despite the cold. Her milk white skin had taken on a yellowish hue. He wasn't good with a needle. He had inflicted a number of deep cuts with a sharp blade, which had bled profusely. He'd stitched the wounds on her thighs and torso and made her body look like a patchwork quilt. But the ones on her face were worse. A deep cut down one cheek, crudely stitched up, had left her face lopsided.

It was a shame. In the beginning she'd been beautiful and had held such promise. He'd truly believed that she was the one. But she was like the rest, ungrateful and fickle. She had wanted more, more than he was prepared to give. In the end, it had been a pleasure to kill her.

It should have been a simple task. All he'd ever wanted was a replacement for Kitty. Pretty young women with blonde hair were everywhere, but still it never worked out right. He slammed his fist into the bench, angry now. Thinking about his wife always upset him. He'd given her everything, made sacrifices, but all she'd done in return was ask for more, and she'd cheated on him. He mustn't think like this. Things were set to change. Bella was different. She would be the one, he felt sure of it.

He'd chosen the final outfit for Bella's predecessor carefully, clothes that would suit her personality. A dress of pale green silk, with a low neckline and a figure hugging skirt. Like all the women that attracted him she had pale, blonde hair. Green suited her, it mirrored her eyes. As he began the slow task of dressing the body, he thought about their time together. This one had been entertaining. In the beginning, when she'd been new, he hadn't held back. But, despite the pain, she hadn't screamed or cried like the first one. This beauty had simply stared at him throughout with those limpid green eyes of hers. She had suffered her pain silently, kept her curses to herself.

He dressed her with care, brushed her long hair and applied a red gloss to her colourless lips. "Goodbye, my dear." He kissed her forehead lightly, lifted her in his arms and walked the few metres to the pit.

* * *

Matt spent the next hour or so digging around in the station evidence archive. The skinned dog incident was at least eighteen months old, and all the evidence was neatly stored away. The problem was, in the interim there had been alterations to the building due to flooding, so everything had been moved.

Finally, his perseverance paid off, and he found the see-through bag containing two dog tags. As expected, one had Marjory Bentley's name and address on it. But she was not the owner. Matt did not remove the tags in case further tests were needed on them. He held the bag up to the light. The name on the second tag was 'Caroline Sheldon.' She lived only a few doors down from the dog sitter.

He decided to call and have a word with this woman first thing in the morning, on his way in. He'd text Lily and tell her. Matt wasn't sure what he'd learn from talking to Caroline Sheldon, but she *was* a piece of the puzzle.

***

It had been a long day. He'd been gone since early morning. It didn't please his mother.

She greeted him with the words, "Dinner is ruined. A shame, because Mrs Hurst did her lamb roast."

"The woman is called Irene, Ma. We will soon be employing many more people. Attitudes will have to change."

"By that you mean mine, Matthew. I'm finding the prospect quite frightening. Strangers all over my property, poking about in the rooms, putting their hands all over our furniture and antiques. God knows what rubbish they will leave lying around the estate. I don't think you have thought it through. It worries me to death. What with that, and your job."

Matt sighed. They'd been over it all so many times. He'd thought she'd be reconciled by now to what was happening to the estate. "My job is fine, I'm fine. I'm not about to take any risks."

"I don't see how you can be fine. How will you cope? They've given you a child as a work partner." She stuck her nose in the air. "And she was chewing gum when you introduced her to me. At the first sign of things getting rough, that one will be off. I know the type."

"You know nothing about her, Ma. Lily has the makings of a good officer. I'd appreciate it if you kept your comments to yourself. You might try dealing with the world as it is, rather than how you would like it to be."

"You have no idea, Matthew. I have a lot to think about. Your job, this house, and the hordes who will come here next year. I worry that we won't have any control over them, and they'll trash the place."

"We will employ security people. The more valuable pieces will be alarmed. The furniture and the cabinets will be roped off. The visitors will be able to look but not touch." He went over it all for the umpteenth time.

"Rope! What use will that be against reprobates who will chance their luck? I'm really not sure about any of this anymore, Matthew. And now Sarah has taken up with that builder friend of yours. They are *down the pub* tonight. I ask you, Matthew, what is she thinking?"

So that was what it was really about — Sarah and Freddie. "Sounds like she's having a good time. Freddie is a lot of fun. She won't come to any harm. It's quiz night at the Fox. If I wasn't so tired, I might have joined them."

"That's not the point. Andrew Denham has set his cap at her. He's not bothered that she's a divorcee with children, and he's got money. Why can't she see sense?"

"Get real, Ma! Sarah can please herself about who she takes up with. She's a big girl. Denham is an old-fashioned fool. Sarah's not for him."

"Olivia rang today. She asked about you." His mother changed the subject.

Olivia Meadows was a young woman that Evelyn Brindle had her eye on as a prospective wife for her son. Matt pulled a face. In his opinion, Olivia was alright in very small doses. But like his mother, she was a snob.

"She's a lovely young woman, and very different from that other one you were so fond of."

"I've told you before, Ma, don't meddle."

"It wasn't me who chased her off, Matthew. But I can't say I was sorry when she went."

"I don't blame you for what happened, Ma. It was my choice to finish with Melissa. But you have to let it be. Both Sarah and I will choose our own partners. If you carry on trying to pair us off, you'll antagonise us and make yourself ill."

"You are not getting any younger. And you're injured. The Meadows family are going to the house in Dorset for a few weeks. Olivia asked if you wanted to join them."

The tone had changed. Evelyn Brindle had put on her best 'wheedling' voice. "Cut out the nonsense, Ma. There's no way I'm going to spend time with that family. Besides, I've got work."

She became brittle again. "Mid-thirties and no woman in your life. I worry about the future, Matthew. I'm not getting any younger. I'd like to see you with an heir in place. You need to settle down, get your priorities right."

His mother left him and went up to bed. By now, Matt had lost his appetite. His mother was never going to change. But her attitude infuriated him.

* * *

Joel Dawson left Bella's house and went to the local supermarket. He pulled into the car park just as Robert drove in behind him. Joel marched up to him. "At times like this Bella needs her friends around her, not people like you. You're continually pestering her. Try leaving her be. She needs to rest."

"What do you mean — people like me? I don't know what you think my role is, but I'm simply advising her, nothing more. Certainly not pestering, as you put it. And I won't be charging a fee either."

"She's not for you," Dawson added. "If you really want to help, get the police to up their game. That boy should have been found by now."

"I totally agree, but everything is not what it seems with the lovely Ms Richards. If you really knew her, you'd know that much."

Joel stared at Robert. "I know enough. You forget, I've known Bella longer than you, and we're friends. She trusts me."

"Then you will know that one of her dodgy little secrets could well be at the bottom of all this."

Joel glowered at him. Bella had hinted at a secret past, and it appeared that Robert knew a great deal more than he did. "You can't take that risk. Get the boy found. Speak to the police. She is going out of her mind with worry."

Robert stared back. "You watch her, don't you? I bet you're not averse to stalking. A pretty lady like Bella, a loner like you. You're weird, d'you know that? Bella isn't safe, and I'm going to warn her."

"You know nothing about our relationship. Bella likes me. We're friends. I don't want you interfering. If you do, I'll get my own back!"

"I hope that's not a threat, Mr Dawson. If it is, I shall be forced to tell the police what you are up to."

Chapter 22

Day 14

Caroline Sheldon lived a few doors along from Marjory Bentley on a side street off Huddersfield Road in Marsden. Matt called there on his way to the station. He was surprised to see the house up for sale. Nonetheless, he banged on the front door.

"Looking for Caroline?" an elderly man called to him from an open window next door. "She's gone. Got a job miles away. She's been gone ages. Estate agent is handling the sale and showing folk round."

Matt flashed his badge at the man. "Did she tell you where she was going? I wanted to talk to her."

"She never said a word. I got up one morning and the house was being cleared. She did leave me a note, said she'd be in touch, but that never happened."

"Is there anyone around who is likely to know?"

"I've no idea who Caroline's friends were. She was the quiet type. It always amazed me that there were no boyfriends. Lovely she was, long legs and blonde hair. She worked at that big builders' merchants on the Marsden

Industrial Park. Someone there might know where she went."

"Did you know Marjory Bentley?"

"Bloody shame what happened to her. Shot she was, but then you'll know that. All she was doing was minding Caroline's dog. I always reckoned she must have disturbed a burglar when she was bringing the dog back that night."

Matt said nothing. Better the elderly man didn't know. He went back to his car and rang Lily at the station.

"I'm off to the industrial park in Marsden. Caroline Sheldon is no longer at the address on the dog tag. She worked for a builders merchants at the park. I'm hoping someone can tell me where she went."

"Want me to meet you there?"

"No, I won't be long. Have another look through the results that have come in. See if there's anything useful."

Marsden Industrial Park was a sprawling area containing both retail and industrial units. The builders merchants the neighbour had referred to — Riley's — was a huge place.

Matt parked his car, and immediately a loud voice boomed at him. "What're you doing here?"

"Freddie! Might ask you the same thing."

Freddie grinned. "Well, I'm working for you. Can't build without bricks and mortar, you know."

"Do you use this place often?"

"I know that tone — it's the cop voice. I come here all the time. Good value and great choice, but even better, it's local."

"Did you know Caroline Sheldon? She used to work here."

"Not really. Stuck-up bitch, she was. Had a run-in with her once about an invoice. She worked in the office and hardly ever ventured out into the warehouse. She's left now. I don't think she's missed."

"Thanks, Freddie. Might see you later if you're still at the house when I get back."

"Won't be, mate. I'm taking Sarah out to dinner. Your mother has reluctantly agreed to babysit."

"Good luck with that. Ma is a past master at scuppering people's plans. Just mind your step."

The warehouse owner and manager, Kevin Riley, remembered Caroline very well. He told Matt that she'd left in a hurry. One week she seemed happy enough, and the next she'd got a job in Glasgow. Left straight away, with no real explanation.

"I was sorry to see her go. She was very good at her job, though I know she wasn't liked. She was too abrasive for most folk. Not surprising that no one's heard from her since."

"Do you know anyone she was close to?"

"That woman who minded the dog. Bad do, what happened there. Murdered, and what was done to that poor dog doesn't bear thinking about."

"Anyone else?"

"Kept herself to herself, did Caroline. But there was a bloke. I remember him because I was surprised. In all the years she'd worked here, I don't recall Caroline having anyone in her life until he turned up. Don't misunderstand me. She was a looker alright, but difficult to get close to — picky and prickly." Riley laughed. "This bloke regularly picked her up from work, and took her out to eat. Doug, his name was. She met him while she was doing jury service in Huddersfield. She told me that he worked at Broadbent's, the paper mill up on yonder hill." He nodded.

"Do you have a surname?"

He shook his head.

"Do you know where Caroline's new job was?" Matt asked.

"She took herself off to Glasgow. A firm called McIntosh Plumbing. Apparently she'd bought into the business. Said she had big plans."

* * *

"Who is he and what the hell have you done to him, Cora? The kid is emaciated!" Cora's sister, Mary, took one look at Oliver Richards and her heart went out to him. He hadn't had a wash in all the time he'd been here. His fine blond hair was dirty and plastered to his head. "Hark at that cough an' all. Where have you been keeping him? In that bloody cellar of ours?"

"You weren't 'ere. Went swanning off on holiday, didn't you? He asked me to keep the lad for a while. Said he'd pay well. He don't need no mollycoddling, Mary. I made 'im a bed up in the cellar. Give 'im a scrap of food and some water every so often. He won't give you any trouble."

"So now you're going away, leaving 'im to me. How long will you be gone, Cora?"

"A week, but I'll see how it goes. You'll cope. Just don't take 'im out. He's been in the papers."

"I don't like this, Cora. Someone might come looking."

"No one is coming all the way up 'ere. You'll get told what to do wi' 'im in a day or two. And don't go getting too fond, 'cause it won't be pretty."

Mary didn't argue. Once Cora was out of the way, she'd sort the lad. The first thing she'd do was warm him up, then give him a long, hot bath. He could do with some different clothes too.

Mary watched her sister drive away, and put a comforting arm around the boy. She had a kind smile. "Let's get you fed and comfortable. Cora's not got an ounce of mothering in her. What do we do about that cough, eh? Do you take medicine for it?"

Oliver Richards nodded. "I have asthma," he wheezed. "I need my inhaler."

"And our Cora never got one for you? Shame on her!"

Mary was angry with her sister. The kid was nothing but a pawn in some game her and that madman were playing. She'd no idea what the boy's fate would be, but she decided to make his time with her as comfortable as she could. To that end, Mary made up a bed on the sofa in front of the sitting room fire. The room was warm, a far cry from the damp cellar he'd been in for the last week. She put the television on, and got him some juice.

He began to cry. "I want my mummy."

"Don't worry, little man. It'll be alright. I'll sort something for that cough." She stroked his head.

"My mummy will wonder where I am."

"You mustn't fret. You're not in any trouble."

Mary's kind words seemed to do the trick, and he began to relax. For the first time in days, the little lad was comfortable. His eyes were closing. Very soon he'd be asleep.

There was a church jumble sale on in the village this afternoon. Mary would nip out. She'd get him something from the chemist for that cough and something to wear from the jumble sale. She'd lock the doors, and there was no phone. She'd only be gone an hour at the most.

* * *

The jumble sale was in the church hall in Meltham. There was plenty of kids' clothing and toys, all of it dirt cheap. Mary picked out a selection for the boy to wear, plus a bagful of toys and games to keep him amused.

Her visit to the chemist did not turn out so well. Mary got into an argument with the pharmacist, who refused to provide her with an inhaler without a doctor's prescription. In the end, she had to settle for a bottle of cough linctus.

* * *

When Matt walked in, Lily looked up with a big smile on her face. "I've been doing some digging, sir. Working on a hunch, I looked at the birth and marriage records again. Guess what I found?"

"Go on, surprise me." He grinned back at her.

"We know that 'Bella Richards' is not her real name. We now have someone in the morgue that we believe was close to her — Agnes Harvey. So I looked up the surname 'Harvey' and struck lucky. One Isabelle Harvey got married in south Manchester six years ago. Guess who to?"

"You think Isabelle is our Bella?"

"Yes I do, it's a shortened version of the name."

"Go on then, who did she marry?"

"Ron Chalker!"

Matt was stunned. If Lily was right, then he could well understand what Bella was doing in witness protection. From what he recalled of the case, Chalker's wife had testified against him. "What makes you so sure you've got the right woman?"

"Because a year later, Isabelle Chalker gave birth to a son — Oliver."

So Bella was hiding from Ronnie Chalker. But was it him who'd taken their son? What was needed now was some straight talking.

"We will go and talk to her. Too much time has passed and there's still nothing on the boy. We need to break this case. Bella knows something. She made a prison visit, and we don't need a crystal ball to tell us who she saw."

Chapter 23

"Tip-off." DS Ian Beckwith stuck his head round Matt's office door. "We sent word round to all the local GPs and pharmacies regarding Oliver Richards's condition. Apparently a woman was in the chemist in Meltham earlier today giving them a hard time because they wouldn't sell her an inhaler. They know this woman, and she does not have a chest condition. What d'you think?"

"I think we should pay her a visit. What's her name?"

"Mary Turnbull. She lives with her sister up on the Holme Road. It's that whitewashed house you see as you reach the top of Scapegoat Hill."

"I know it, sir," Lily called out. "I'll drive if you want."

They left the station and made for the road out towards Holmfirth. From there they would take the Woodhead Road and head for the village of Holme. The countryside was beautiful, but it would take a while to get there.

"If she lives in Holme, why go to Meltham for a chemist?" Matt asked.

Lily smiled. "It is a bit of a drive, isn't it? Perhaps she had other stuff to do there. There is still a bank in Meltham. At the rate they're closing, it brings people in from miles around.

"Whereabouts do you live, Lily?"

"I live in Marsden, in one of those cottages on the hillside above the canal. I was lucky, got it at a good price about five years ago. An elderly couple had it. They were moving into a sheltered flat."

"What about your parents?"

"My father did one when I was a kid, so I never had much to do with him. He still turns up from time to time, but he's a waste of space. Does nowt but cause trouble. My mum's a bit flaky too. There has been a string of men, most of them wanting a roof over their heads more than anything else. When I was little, I spent a lot of time with my grandparents. But they're both dead now."

"Is your mum still around?"

Lily gave him a sidelong glance. "Oh yes. You're bound to bump into her sooner or later. Sadie Haines, the parish's wild woman."

"I'm sorry. I had no idea. You've had a difficult time." Matt was shocked. Lily seemed so down to earth and, well, normal.

"It's okay. I can take care of myself. I've had to for most of my life. What about you? Life on your country estate all sunshine and roses?"

Matt grinned. "With a mother like mine? Hardly!"

"She loves you, though. She cares, and that goes a long way. What about your dad?"

Matt looked sad for a moment. "I lost my dad when I was in my late twenties. It was a big change for both of us, and my ma has never got over it. It was a great pity. I wish I could have spent more time with him, but I was sent off to a private boarding school in Leeds when I was quite young. I was hardly ever at home."

"I'm sorry, I don't mean to pry. You must think I'm a right nosey so and so."

"I'm a bit like you on that score. I like my personal life to stay that way. But when you're working with someone all the time, you can't help finding out something about each other."

The Holme Road snaked its way for miles through the hills and across the moors. Finally they drove through Holme village and reached the lane that climbed up Scapegoat Hill. They could see the cottage standing alone on the left.

"Looks almost derelict," Matt noted. "They can't have had any repairs done for years."

Lily checked her phone and read a text from the station. "Two sisters live here, Cora and Mary Mason. Nothing known about either of them."

Matt was edgy. Time and place had shifted, slightly out of kilter. He stared out at the old cottage, built of whitewashed stone. Sitting there in stark profile against the hillside, it looked just like that other house. That too had been out in the sticks, and just as ramshackle. Even the paintwork was the same colour, a dark rural green.

Lily glanced at him but made no comment. "I'll go and knock, sir." Matt hung back, his stomach doing somersaults. He tried to remind himself — *This is not the same place,. All that is done with now.*

"No answer, unless they are deliberately keeping quiet."

"Perhaps she's not back yet. I'll go round the back." But Matt hesitated still.

This was what he had been dreading. A panic attack just when he needed to stay on top. The boy could be here. Why else would Mary Mason want an inhaler so urgently? The pharmacist reckoned that neither she nor her sister had needed anything like that before. His instinct was at it again.

Lily called out to him. "I've had another text from the nick, sir. Apparently Mary Mason went to the church jumble sale in Meltham and bought a load of boy's clothes and games. Looks like we've struck gold."

The back door was locked. Matt joined Lily at the front. She was peering in through a grimy downstairs window.

"I can't see very well, but there is definitely someone in there, lying on the sofa in front of the fire."

Matt had a look. She was right. He banged on the door again. Nothing.

"Round the back. I'll kick it in." He darted off. The back door was the usual cheap plywood. He swung his good leg, gave it a hefty kick and it swung open. They were in.

It wasn't just the outside, the interior, too, reminded him of that other place. Matt stood in the kitchen, transfixed. Only his eyes moved, darting from corner to stone walled corner. It was a dead ringer for that other kitchen, almost bare of utensils. The walls began to close in around him and he was finding it difficult to breathe. He felt as if all the air was being sucked out of his lungs. Motes of dust spiralled around in the odd shaft of sunlight that managed to get through the dirty window. The light was strange, unnatural. He began to sway, he was going to fall to the ground. In his head, he heard a noise, and then a scream. For one crazy moment he could smell the burning after the grenade fell.

Lily was shaking his arm. "Sir! Sir! Are you alright? You've gone dead white."

Matt bent double, clutching his knees. His mouth was open and he gasped for breath. "No. I'm terrified!" It was no good pretending, Lily could see the state he was in.

She spoke to him gently. "It's okay. You're safe. This isn't the same place."

"I know, I know. But this is how it takes me." He drew in a deep breath. This was a full-blown panic attack.

The only way to deal with it was to let it run its course. He wiped at the cold sweat on his forehead. He was powerless to make it stop. He tried to take deep breaths.

Precious seconds ticked by. "Let's have a look around. It might take your mind off it," Lily suggested at last. "The sofa . . ."

He stumbled after her through the hallway and into the sitting room. He couldn't think. He'd even forgotten why they were here. Then he heard the coughing.

Lily grabbed his arm. "That doesn't sound good."

The sitting room was warm. There was a log fire roaring away. A small shape lay on the sofa, covered by a duvet. Matt lifted a corner. Oliver Richards was white, and he was shaking. Every few seconds a harsh cough interrupted his breathing. Matt could tell that the lad had a temperature. He touched the boy's arm.

"Olly," he whispered, "You're safe now. Time to wake up." Matt turned to Lily. "He isn't well at all. Ring for an ambulance, and we'll need a forensic team up here too."

Chapter 24

Superintendent Dyson patted Matt on the back. "You did good. Kid's doing okay in hospital, and Alison Wray has taken the mother to see him."

Matt shook his head. "Wasn't down to me. We got a tip-off and simply followed it up."

Matt didn't mention his panic attack. On the drive back, Lily had assured him she wasn't about to tell anyone either. If he was lucky, they'd get less severe once he got accustomed to the job again.

"Beckwith arrested Mary Mason in Meltham. The other one, her sister Cora, will be apprehended soon. Apparently she has gone to Scarborough to visit an aunt."

"The sisters didn't take the boy. I'll lay odds on it."

"You could be right. In her statement, Mary Mason told Beckwith that they were minding him for a friend. Trouble is, she won't say who that friend is." Dyson stuck his hands in his pockets and rocked on his heels. "But she will, once she comes to her senses."

"Forensics?"

"Scouring the cottage as we speak. What're you up to now?"

"I'm following up on a hunch," said Matt. "Given that both the blue stamp victims were linked to Bella, I'm checking out links between the others. The green stamp killings, for example — there were three of them. I'm checking whether they knew or had dealings with a woman called Caroline Sheldon. She owned the skinned dog. I'm trying to trace the woman."

"Why? What's her part in all this?"

Matt looked at the superintendent. "I think she was the person the killer was really after. I think the reason for the three green stamp murders was to get rid of anyone who was close to Caroline. When he took her, he didn't want her nearest and dearest coming to us."

"That's a giant leap! How d'you work that one out?"

"Because I can't find Caroline. It's as if she melted into thin air. And at least one of the green stamp victims, Marjory Bentley, was close to her. She would certainly have beaten a path to our door if Caroline suddenly went AWOL with no word. Caroline was supposed to have gone to work in Glasgow. Allegedly she bought shares in a firm called McIntosh Plumbing. The firm exists alright, but Caroline isn't there. They have never heard of her. If the move had been genuine, Caroline would have maintained contact with Margery. Might even have wanted her to visit. That is why Margery had to be got rid of. Don't forget, we now have a link to the 'Mr Apology' killings and what has happened to Bella's son. I strongly suspect she is his intended next victim."

Dyson shook his head. "This Caroline has to be somewhere. There will have been some mistake. Who did you get the info from?"

"Her old employer, Kevin Riley, the chap who owns the builder's merchants on Marsden Industrial Estate. And I don't think he got it wrong."

"Do we know what she looks like, this Caroline Sheldon?"

"I'm getting a photo emailed over from her old work place." Matt paused for a moment. "Since we have this new information, I'd like to speak to the 'Mr Apology' team. Bring them all up to speed."

"It's Carlisle's case."

"Yes, I know, but he isn't getting anywhere, is he, sir?"

"Fair comment! But I foresee trouble ahead." Dyson stalked out of the office.

Matt lifted the phone and called Kevin Riley.

"DI Matt Brindle, Huddersfield CID." It was tripping off the tongue more easily now. "Would you recognise this Doug person if I showed you a couple of photos?"

"Yes, I think so. He was an odd one. Smartly dressed, but didn't say much. Not the type I imagined Caroline would go for at all. I did ask her about him, but she was cagey. At one point I began to think he had some sort of hold over her, not that I had any idea what that could be."

"I'll bring a couple of photos round a little later." This didn't sound like their tattoo man, though. Once Oliver Richards was up to it, he'd ask the boy about him.

The next part of the puzzle was to look at the red stamp murders, and try to ascertain if a particular individual was linked to those. The files were on Carlisle's desk. Matt went to ask if he could borrow them.

Carlisle handed them over. "Heard you want a conference. Won't get you anywhere. We've done all we can."

"Another angle has presented itself," said Matt. "I thought it would be pertinent to tell the team."

"Whatever. Dyson has called the meet for six. But make it snappy, will you? The missus has got folk coming round tonight."

Back at his desk, Matt looked at the profiles of the two red stamp victims. They were a couple, Carl and Deborah Thornley. Both of them had been found up on Marsden Moor thirteen months ago, shot in the head. The profile Carlisle and his team had put together was sketchy at best. Carl Thornley had been a partner in a dental practice in Huddersfield. His wife had been the nurse. Matt would visit first thing in the morning.

Of the three green stamp victims, Margery Bentley they already knew about. One of the other two was Oscar Firth, a student at the local university. He had worked part-time at an Italian restaurant on Marsden High Street. Matt knew it. Firth had been found in his car in the university car park, shot in the temple. The last victim was Sonia Crosland, a hairdresser who had lived and worked in Huddersfield. She was unmarried and lived alone. Sonia had been found dead in her flat. Matt needed to check what their relationship was to Caroline.

The email from Kevin Riley at the builder's merchants had arrived. Matt sent the photo straight to the printer and waited.

Lily returned from the canteen with a cup of coffee for him. "What do you intend to tell the others tonight? You should know that the sniping has already started. Beckwith is telling anyone who'll listen that you're Dyson's new favourite and to watch out. They are also saying that you and me won't last. They say I'm working with you temporarily and you'll get rid the minute you're able to. They're calling us 'chalk and cheese.'"

Matt got up from his desk to fetch the printout. "That's a bit childish, and he's wrong. I haven't made up my mind about the job yet, Lily. Some of what they are saying is true. I am giving the job a trial, and the super placed you with me until I make up my mind. So nothing is certain. But if I do decide to stay, I think you'd make an excellent member of my team."

"Thank you, sir, I'm chuffed with that. I know it's just gossip, but I will pass on whatever I hear. I shouldn't tell tales, but DI Carlisle has a vindictive streak. Beckwith's not bad, but he follows Carlisle's lead."

But Matt wasn't listening. He was staring at the picture of Caroline Sheldon. He held it up for Lily to see. "Who does she remind you of?"

"Good Heavens! I see what you mean. That blonde hair, the pretty features. She's a ringer for Bella Richards."

"So, he's got a type. Our killer is particular. The women he targets look like this." Matt held up the image again. "No doubt it's his idea of perfection. But they only become targets if they lead insular lives. No good going after someone with a husband, loads of family and a wide circle of friends. They'd make a lot of noise when she disappeared. As it is, the women I suspect he has taken have not even been reported to us as missing — like Caroline. Bella fits the bill. She has very few people in her life. Think about it. If it weren't for the fact she's in witness protection, who would notice if she disappeared too?"

Lily nodded. "Her son. And your interest was sparked because of Alan Fisher."

"That was the killer's mistake, trying to deal with her son. Sending the letter purporting to be from Gabe Parker."

"Why not just kill the boy?"

"I don't know, but given time he might have done. He might have been waiting until he'd taken Bella. Maybe he wanted to use the lad as some sort of bargaining chip. We need to check if there is anyone else who knew Caroline well. Relatives. Anyone she might have discussed this new man with."

"And the randoms?"

"If I am right, they are far from random, Lily. Our killer is getting rid of anyone who might interfere with his plans."

Chapter 25

Superintendent Dyson had told everyone to attend the meeting, and the main office was packed. Carlisle and Beckwith were there, with a number of uniformed officers, plus a third team that Matt hadn't yet got to know.

There was a lot of chatter. The teams were discussing the case, and the atmosphere was tense. Carlisle stood with his arms folded, his eyes fastened on Matt. His gaze was hostile.

Dyson rapped on the table. "Keep it down, you lot. Regarding the 'Mr Apology' killings, things 'ave happened. Evidence is starting to stack up that suggests links where previously we didn't see any. That's down to the fresh eyes of DI Brindle here. We also have the possibility of other victims we don't know about. Originally, DI Carlisle had the case mostly to himself, but in light of what we now know that will have to change."

Matt saw the look Carlisle threw Dyson's way. The DI didn't like it one bit.

Dyson addressed Carlisle. "The case has grown too big. There's only you and Beckwith, and with all the new evidence, the two of you will never manage." The super paused. The room had fallen silent. "I've decided to take up the role of SIO myself once again."

Very diplomatic, thought Matt.

"So the lot of you will report any findings to me. We will collate all information on that board there." He pointed to a huge incident board set up in the main office. "Since the new stuff has come from investigations carried out by DI Brindle, he is going to explain what we have so far."

Matt moved to the front of the room beside Dyson, and cleared his throat. "Right. The 'Mr Apology' killer. When DI Carlisle's team found that photo of Oliver Richards in Agnes Harvey's house, it gave us our link. What we didn't understand then was what it meant." He pinned up the photo of Caroline Sheldon next to Bella Richards' on the incident board. "We know more now. These two women are not only a similar age and live similar lives, but they look alike too. I believe our killer is not primarily interested in those people we have been referring to as 'randoms.' It is a female close to them that is his main target."

There was a buzz around the room. Carlisle was shaking his head. "Where did you get this nonsense from?" he called out.

Matt ignored him and wrote the names 'Margery Bentley,' 'Oscar Firth' and 'Sonia Crosland' on the board. "These are the three victims that have green stamps on their arms. I believe they all knew Caroline Sheldon, and were all close to her in some way. Had she disappeared, they would have raised the alarm and reported her missing, so they had to go."

"Where's your proof, Brindle?" Carlisle shouted. "Sounds like a bloody good fairy story, but we'll need more than one of your hunches to move this forward."

There was muttering.

Dyson stepped forward, and his voice boomed out, silencing the talk. "I think DI Brindle's theory has merit.

Let's face it, we've got sod all else, so we'll make it a priority to check these three out. Talk to the staff at the firm Caroline worked for here. Check out Crosland and Firth for links to her." Dyson nodded at Carlisle. "You and DC Beckwith can see to that."

Matt took over again. "Thanks, sir. Those victims found with red stamps need checking out too." He wrote 'Carl and Deborah Thornley' on the board. "Look again at their lives, who they knew. They worked in a dental practice in town. We need the name of a missing female to go with this pair." He tapped the board. "The intended victim behind these two killings will look like Caroline and Bella: blonde and pretty, but more importantly, she won't have been reported as missing."

Carlisle grunted. "Very helpful. We're back to chasing bloody shadows again."

"Not if we're thorough. Check back, ask the right questions, and I'm sure we'll find a female the Thornleys were close to that fits the profile. Back to Caroline. Until we know differently, she is missing. I have followed up on the information I was given by her former employer and drawn a blank. We must extend our enquiries. She was seeing a man shortly before she disappeared. All I have is the name 'Doug.' I will show her employer the photo of the man who abducted Oliver Richards, and see if he recognises him. Speaking of Oliver, Mary Mason has been apprehended but her sister, Cora Mason, is still out there. She needs finding and bringing in. It goes without saying that it would help matters enormously if they told us who they were minding the child for."

The chatter started once more, but the smile had gone from Carlisle's face.

Dyson's voice boomed out again. "Good. You all know what needs doing, so go and do it."

* * *

The tears poured down Bella's cheeks. She couldn't help it. Her intense relief on hearing the news about Oliver had opened the floodgates. When the officer knocked on her door and gave her the news, she broke down. He had reassured her, and said Oliver was safe, but Bella insisted on seeing him for herself. The officer had taken her to the hospital.

Her son was asleep, but tossing and turning in his sleep. He looked flushed. His tousled, blond hair was spread across the pillow.

A nurse was sitting with him. "Don't worry, he's fine. We've given him something so he will sleep for several hours."

Bella pulled a chair close to the bed. Her tiny boy had a drip in his arm. "Is he . . . injured?" Her voice trembled.

"A few scratches, but nothing serious," said the nurse. "It's his chest that is giving concern. We know he has asthma, but he has an infection too. That's why he's on the drip. We can give him fluids and antibiotics that way."

Bella took hold of his hand and stroked his brow. Olly slept on. Part of her had believed that she'd never see her boy again, but the police had been true to their word. They'd found him for her. "Can I stay?"

The nurse smiled and nodded. "He is safe now. There is an officer on guard outside. No one will get near him again."

Bella smiled in relief, but the tears kept coming.

Chapter 26

Day 15

"Today we speak to Oliver Richards," Matt said.

Lily looked doubtful. "Provided his mum and the doctors are okay with that, sir. The lad has been through a lot. Poor little bugger. He might not be up to going through it all just yet."

"Don't worry, I'll check with his mum first. In the meantime we'll visit the builders' merchants, and speak to Kevin Riley again. We'll show him the photo of the tattooed man, and see if he recognises him."

"I thought Carlisle had that gig?" Lily said.

"We've met Riley. Carlisle is chasing Caroline from a different angle."

Lily was silent for a moment. "What about Broadbent's paper mill? Someone there might know him."

"If this Doug did take Caroline, I doubt he's been anywhere near Broadbent's. That will have been a cover. But we'll ask, just to make absolutely sure."

"Carlisle's team aren't happy. Beckwith's been gossiping about you. He was going at it like a bloody fishwife when I got 'ere this morning. Clammed up when he saw me."

Matt smiled. "It's to be expected. I'm new — well, as far as they are concerned, I am. More than half of the people who work here now weren't around when I was active before. So they don't think of me as one of them. They probably reckon I'm Dyson's pet, what with him giving me a chunk of the case and us being so friendly."

Lily smiled. "Why is that, sir?"

"Dyson had a thing for my mother a few years back. He was always around. Took her out a few times."

Lily laughed. "The super and your mother? I can't see that at all. He's a bit of a div where women are concerned. Never gets it right."

"And he didn't on this occasion either. My mother is a snob. The only thing Talbot had going for him was his rank in the force. At the time, he was tipped for ACC. Unfortunately a heart attack put paid to that. Every year since then they have tried to retire him. It's only sheer stubbornness that keeps him going."

"So no ACC, no romance, sir?"

"That's about the size of it, Lily. My dear mother dropped him like a hot brick the minute he became ill."

"You two seen the morning paper?" DC Beckwith came over to Matt's desk. He stood there smirking, holding a newspaper. "This'll really stir things up."

Matt hadn't reckoned with this at all. Ron Chalker's face was splashed right across the front page. The article also carried a smaller, inset photo of Bella and their son, Oliver. Chalker had gone to the paper complaining that his boy had been snatched and he hadn't been told. The paper had obviously lapped it up, and then gone in search of Bella. They'd put two and two together, and found her.

Matt wondered if she knew. She'd not admitted to being in witness protection, but her whereabouts and new identity were well and truly blown now.

"Chalker's missus, who'd have thought it? She's lucky to get the boy back. Half the North West's underworld have a beef with that villain."

Beckwith had a point, but then he didn't know about the threat to Bella from Chalker himself.

Lily was already on the phone. She shook her head at him. "She's gone to the hospital to be with her son."

Of course she had. What else would she do? "We need to tell her straight away. Hospital first, and then the builders' merchants."

* * *

Bella had fallen asleep holding Olly's hand. She was still in her chair, slumped forward over his bed. A tap on the shoulder startled her awake.

It was the last person she was expecting to see. "James! Why are you here? What's happened?"

He handed her a rolled-up newspaper. "Read this."

Bella sat up. It had to be something important to bring James here. She looked at the front page and her heart sank. This. Just when things were getting better. She looked at James. "How did this happen?"

James shook his head. "It's down to Chalker. I told you he'd use your visit for his own ends. When you left he contacted his solicitor and told him about your son. He complained that he hadn't been told. Reckoned that if you hadn't gone to see him, he still wouldn't know. The rest, about you and Oliver, is down to a tenacious reporter, some bright spark looking to make a name for himself. Once the press got hold of the kidnap story, they pieced it together."

"Does Ronnie know where we are?"

"Yes, I suspect he does. I did warn you that he would try something."

Bella looked at him. "It was just a simple visit."

"It was hardly that. By telling him about Oliver, you gave him exactly what he needed to find you." James shook his head.

"I had to tell him about Olly. That was the whole purpose of the visit. Does this mean we have to move again?"

"It's my job to keep you safe, Bella. I can't do that if Chalker knows about your new identity, and where you live."

"I want to think about it. I can't go anywhere yet, Olly isn't up to it. He has a chest infection, and they want to keep him in for a while."

James stared at her. "But you do understand the danger?"

She nodded.

"Chalker is a vindictive criminal."

"You don't have to tell me that," she snapped back. "Did you find anything out about his accident?"

"He wasn't lying. He did suffer a skull fracture. But the bit about being a changed man is doubtful. People in the prison reckon he is as bad as ever."

Bella was looking at the newspaper. "Once Olly is better, I'll consider it. There is nothing to keep me here now. I've lost Alan and my aunt. No one will want to know us once they've read this." She handed it back to James. "No matter what we've been through, we'll still be seen as the wife and son of a murderer. A new start might be just what we need."

* * *

Bella was sitting with a sleeping Oliver when Matt and Lily arrived. She didn't look pleased to see them.

"Don't wake him up. He needs the rest."

Matt smiled at her. "We didn't come here to talk to Oliver, although we will have to sooner or later. It's you we've come to see."

Bella sighed wearily. "You've seen the article. I've already had a visit from my witness protection contact. He wants to move us again and I've said yes. Once Olly is through the worst, we will go. We'll disappear again."

"You admit that you are in the programme?"

She shrugged. "It's pointless pretending otherwise now. My cover is blown. That rag gives it all, chapter and verse. I'm the wife of a murdering villain — Ronnie Chalker no less. We can't stay here now."

Matt touched her shoulder briefly. "I'll make sure you and the boy are not left alone."

She nodded. "There is an officer in the corridor. I feel safe enough in here."

"We have arrested one of the two women who were holding Oliver, but we suspect that someone else was behind his kidnap. Has he said anything?" Matt asked.

"No. Olly has been out of it for most of the time."

"If it's any consolation, the woman we have in custody was in Meltham buying clothing and toys for him. She was trying to get him an inhaler when she was caught."

"It's something, I suppose. But it wasn't a woman who took him. He hasn't said anything about his ordeal, but he's been rambling in his sleep. It was a man. He had long hair and tattoos. Olly remembers them well enough."

Chapter 27

Chalker! He slammed the newspaper down onto the table in disgust. Surely Chalker wasn't looking for sympathy? A more vicious criminal you couldn't find in these parts. But it meant that Bella was now a focus of attention. National attention. He closed his eyes, suddenly weary. This was far more difficult than the others had been. The woman could never simply disappear and no one notice. Not now.

His plans would have to change. He read through the headline again. Maybe it wasn't all bad. From what he'd heard about Chalker, the man was a vindictive sod. Now he knew where Bella was, Chalker might use that information to get his revenge. He smiled. It could certainly be made to look that way. It was the obvious way around his dilemma. In fact, it was perfect. It worked to his advantage. Bella would disappear and Chalker would get the blame for organising it. He would lay out a trail. If he did it right, the police would look no further than Bella's ex. He was back on track, and so close he could taste success.

He had been ready for days now. The house was spick and span, all prepared for the next occupant. The last chosen one had gone into the pit, little left of her by now but bones. With Bella in his sights, he wasn't sorry. Caroline had been like the first one, Anita. Rebellious. So he'd had to teach her a lesson. Unfortunately, he had gone too far again. He'd inflicted serious injuries and was obliged to put her out of her misery. Her death had not come easily. The only thing he could do was imprison her, keep her chained to that bench in the cold and damp without anything to ease the discomfort. The cuts had bled a lot. Her last hours had been excruciating. Poor Caroline! How she had suffered.

She had been painfully thin at the end. For weeks he'd given her only crusts and water, and she was emaciated. The slow-burning peat fire on the floor of the pit would soon reduce his blonde beauty to a charred skeleton. Once the pit cooled, he'd put her with Anita, under the slate floor he was laying in the kitchen.

* * *

"You again." Riley didn't look pleased to see Matt and Lily.

Matt took out the photo. "I want you to look at this. Tell me if you recognise the man."

"Be sharp, we've got the auditors in. Everything's fine, I'm sure, but the process still makes me nervous."

Matt handed him the enhanced still from the video that Luke Standish had taken on his mobile. Riley studied it for a few seconds.

"I see what you mean. It could be him. But Caroline's bloke had shorter hair, and no hat."

Matt passed him a second image. "We've had the tattoos on his arms blown up."

Riley shook his head. "No. The bloke who was seeing Caroline had no tattoos. I would have remembered."

"You're sure?" Matt asked, disappointed.

"Yes, positive. He was just a regular bloke, nothing odd or different about him at all."

They walked back to the car.

"What d'you think?" Lily asked.

"I don't know what to think. If this is the man we're after, where have the tattoos gone?"

"He could have worn a disguise when he took the boy, sir. They could have been false tats. A wig would be simple enough to get hold of. That way he's had us running around looking at all the wrong folk. My neighbour's kid has got some transfer things. They look just like tats. She puts them on her arms, a different design every day."

Matt looked at the photo again. "You could be right. That hair could be a wig. Perhaps the tattoos are false too."

"Want to find out if this Doug does work at Broadbent's?"

"No. You can ring them from the station when we get back. It's more important to look at Carl and Deborah Thornley. Find out if anyone they were close to hasn't been seen in a while."

* * *

Oliver Richards woke up and found his mother dozing beside him. He stroked her cheek gently. It was something he did in the morning if he'd been sleeping in her bed. Bella awoke and held him close, nuzzling his hair.

"You had me scared to death," she whispered. "I thought I'd never see you again."

Oliver coughed. "It was the man. He said he had some comics and I could have them. I'm sorry, Mummy."

Bella kissed him. "It isn't your fault. The doctor says your cough is getting better. I'll take you home with me just as soon as they let me."

"The man was okay, he didn't hurt me. But I didn't like the lady." His voice was croaky. "She locked me up and she said nasty things. She said I wouldn't see you again."

Oliver began to cry. It had been a terrible ordeal. Bella knew she was lucky to have him back. She had to keep him safe now.

"We are going to move away," she told him. "To a place where naughty people won't bother us."

Oliver smiled back. The idea seemed to please him.

"Bella?"

It was Robert Nolan. Bella looked up and smiled at him.

"How's your son? Is he recovering?"

"Yes, but he's very tired. I'm staying here with him. I don't want to let him out of my sight."

"If you want to go home and change, I can arrange something. There is a police officer outside, and I can get a nurse to sit with him."

"It's a nice idea. I must look a mess. I've not moved from his side since yesterday."

He smiled. "I didn't mean it like that. I'm sure Oliver is quite safe in here."

Bella stroked her son's forehead. He was sleeping again. "Okay, an hour won't make much difference. I can have a shower and get a change of clothes. That detective was here earlier, Brindle. He wants to talk to Olly, but I'm scared it will spook him — you know, re-living it all again. Can you do something?"

"Yes, I'll have a word, make him wait."

Bella smiled. "Thank you, Robert. I knew you'd sort it."

"I'll drop you off at your home. I have something to do, so I'll give you a ring and let you know when I'm coming to pick you up."

Bella liked Robert. He was a considerate man. Had things been different, he could have been a good friend.

They drove out of the hospital. "The police are still investigating, and still getting nowhere," Robert told her. "They need to sharpen up. I hope they are not relying on getting evidence from Oliver. It's been several days, and he's been ill. He won't remember much. They still haven't apprehended the other sister, the one who was holding him."

"To be honest, Robert, I don't care. Oliver is safe, and that's all that matters to me."

Chapter 28

Lily hurried over to Matt's desk. "I've dug out the files on Carl and Deborah Thornley. Problem is, they seem so ordinary. He was a partner in a dental practice and she was the nurse. The Thornleys lived in the flat above their work. Not very glamorous, but it is in a nice part of town, just outside Huddersfield on the Halifax Road. There are some big houses out that way. The other people who work there were interviewed at the time, but they couldn't tell us much."

Matt sighed. Interesting, but not enough. They needed to know a lot more about the pair. They had to find that elusive someone they'd known, and who had also disappeared. "Relatives?" he asked.

"Deborah's mother lives local. We could talk to her. She will know more about them than their colleagues."

"It's a start. Find her number and make an appointment for this afternoon. We need a name to go with the red stamp killings."

DC Ian Beckwith strode into the office. "Cora Mason has been found."

"Good. I need a serious talk with her!"

"Sorry, DI Brindle, I should have made myself clearer. She's been found dead. Shot in the temple and left in Linfit Woods. Forensics are on it, and I'm heading out there now to take a look."

Obviously someone didn't want Cora Mason to talk, and from the way she'd been murdered, it sounded like their killer. "Does her sister know?" Brindle asked.

Beckwith nodded. "Yes, and she's distraught. We're still holding her, and the doctor had to be called. Reckons she can't help. Has no idea who would do such a thing."

"She knows alright. Distraught or not, we need the name of the man who took the boy to them."

Lily put the phone down. "Deborah's mum, Sarah Baxter, says we can go round this afternoon. Oh, and one interesting little titbit — Carl Thornley's cousin was Anita Verity." Matt looked blank. "You know — the model. Moved to London and made it big. Used to be in all the papers, then, for reasons she wouldn't disclose, she gave it all up and came home. The press hounded her for ages. Finally they printed a story about her being depressed after breaking up with some footballer. After that, she became a recluse. Sarah Baxter told me because she thought that was why I was calling. She thought we might have found her. Apparently Anita and Carl were close. Sarah Baxter is concerned that Anita might not know that Carl is dead. She wasn't at the funeral, and didn't get in touch."

A recluse! That would fit the killer's spec to a T. "Do we have a photo?" Matt asked.

"I'll find one. Shouldn't be difficult." Lily googled Anita Verity and sent the image she'd found to the printer. "Sir, you need to see this. Just our killer's type."

Matt took the image from her. It showed another pretty blonde, just like Caroline and Bella.

* * *

Bella had showered, changed and was having a bite to eat when the front doorbell rang. She was expecting

Robert, come to take her back to the hospital. But it was Joel Dawson.

"I had to see you. Make sure you're okay."

He looked anxious. The half-hearted attempt at a beard had gone, leaving his face looking thin and pale. Bella gave him a smile. "Now Olly is safe and sound, I'm fine, Joel. I'm just about to go back to the hospital to sit with him. Robert is picking me up. I thought you were him, actually."

"You don't need him. Let me take you."

"Robert doesn't mind. Anyway, you've got work."

"I've taken a few days off. I couldn't settle, Bella. I saw the papers and I was far too worried about you."

Bella spoke firmly. "You shouldn't jeopardise your job because of me. You know what they're like. Take too much time off, and they'll find a way of getting rid."

Joel shook his head, as if to dismiss her words. "Have you stopped for a moment to consider what is happening? Do you realise that you are at the centre of something big? First Alan, then your son. The paper wrote that the woman they found dead the other day was your aunt. Bella, I've been going out of my mind. I worry that the killer will come after you next. The paper reckons it's your ex-husband who is behind this. He holds you responsible for him being put away, and he wants revenge. You are in grave danger. I don't understand why the police aren't doing more. At the very least they should be standing guard. Someone should be on duty at your door now. I couldn't stand it if anything happened to you. I don't think you realise how important you are to me."

Bella's heart sank. Not this again. She knew Joel liked her, and she liked him, just not in that way. Better to get it out in the open. "Look, Joel, don't get too attached. I'm not in as much danger as you seem to think. It isn't my ex who is doing this, but just to be safe, I'm making plans to leave the area. I'll go somewhere where he can't find me so easily. So I won't be around for much longer."

Joel looked horrified. "You're running away again. I know what you're up against. I want to help. You and Olly don't have to leave. You can move in with me. I'll keep you both safe."

Bella shook her head. "No! It wouldn't work. I have to disappear. I have to consider our safety, mine and Olly's. Anyway, no one will want to know me around here now. I'm the wife of a convicted murderer, Joel. Better I make a fresh start."

"I hoped we would have a future together. You must know how I feel."

Bella sighed. This was getting out of hand. "No, Joel. You have to forget about me. Go back to work, and put me out of your head."

Her mobile buzzed. "That will be Robert texting me. He's picking me up."

"I can do that. I'll take you anywhere you want. Get rid of him. I'll come to the hospital and sit with you both. Robert is no good for you."

Bella shook her head. "You can't say that, it's not true. Robert is a good man. He's been a great help. Please, Joel, just go and leave me alone."

Joel looked away. "I don't like the creep. There's something weird about him."

"That's rich, Joel, coming from you!" Bella was losing it. She hadn't had much sleep, and she was tired of Joel's persistence. Why wouldn't he just leave her alone?

He stepped closer. "What do you mean? I'm not weird. I'm your friend. I care. I'm simply trying to look out for you."

"You watch me. You're always in the background somewhere, spying. Every time I turn round, you're there. The minute I think I'm free, you're back again. It isn't Robert who's weird, Joel, it's you. You're the creepy one. I've thought that for ages, so do other people. Now please go. I don't want you here!"

Bella had shouted the last words. Joel looked shocked. But she had to say it. Robert was the one who'd help her. He'd known Alan, and he'd stepped in when she'd needed someone. Joel was okay in small doses, but he needed keeping at arm's length.

He stood very straight and looked her in the eye. Bella stepped back. "If that's how you feel, I'll go. But you will be sorry for this, Bella. Very soon you'll wish you hadn't said those things. You will regret the way you've treated me."

Chapter 29

They'd parked outside a big stone house.

Matt nodded at the sign on the gate. "The dental practice is still going."

"That'll be Carl Thornley's partner running it," said Lily. "He was interviewed at the time. Didn't know much. Carl didn't turn up for work one day and he was never seen again. As far as the partner was aware, there were no problems. The Thornleys were happily married and had no debts."

Matt frowned. "So which one of the Thornleys' friends was he really after, our killer?"

"Deborah's mother lives on the estate over there. She might know something that will help."

"Okay, let's get it over with. I hate dragging stuff up like this. The poor woman is probably just getting her head together, then we come along and bring it all back again."

"When I spoke to her on the phone, she sounded fine."

Matt doubted that. Whatever impression she'd given, she'd lost a daughter, and the killer was still at large. She'd be a long way from fine.

Sarah Baxter was in her early fifties, tall, with short brown hair.

Matt introduced them. "Sorry to do this, Mrs Baxter. We would like to talk to you about Deborah and Carl."

Sarah Baxter opened the door for them. "I'm not sure what I can tell you that hasn't already been said. Carl was a dentist, and Deb was his nurse. It was a lucrative business, kept them in new cars and foreign holidays. They had no enemies. They were just ordinary. Why are you here now? Has something happened?"

"The case is ongoing, Mrs Baxter," Matt explained. "We are looking into a different aspect of it."

"Did they see much of Anita Verity?" asked Lily.

"She was Carl's cousin. She lived locally. A pretty girl, but troubled, you know how they can get. Always on a diet, never thin enough. She used to come round here with them and barely touch her food. Then I read the lurid tales in the press. Anita had an affair with a Premier League footballer. He finished it, and Anita really came unstuck. She couldn't get her head straight after that. For a while she leaned a little too hard on Carl and Deb. Then she disappeared."

She sighed and shook her head. "It makes me want to weep. Such a waste. Not only my Deb and Carl, but what that girl Anita did with the chances she had. She was a clever girl, you know. Spent a couple of years at university doing law. She spent hours at the courthouse in Huddersfield. I was really surprised when Deb told me she was taking up modelling instead." Sarah Baxter took a tissue and dabbed at her eyes. "Why? Has Anita got something to do with Carl and Deb's murders? The police who came before never asked about her."

"We are following a number of new leads, Mrs Baxter. We know our killer was responsible for a number of deaths, Carl and Deborah's among them. But they were not alone. There were others that we know nothing about."

"Surely that wouldn't happen. Their bodies would be found. If not, then someone would report them missing," she replied, puzzled.

"For that to happen they would need to have people close to them who would notice. Granted it is a very risky strategy for a killer. He has taken risks. We do not know enough about him. It might be that killing his true target's nearest and dearest is simply part of some insane ritual," Matt explained. "We are dealing with a serial killer. The reasons why he commits the crimes will be complex."

"And you think she can help — Anita?"

Matt nodded.

"I did have an address for her. She was on my Christmas card list. Give me a minute, and I'll see if I can find it."

She disappeared into an adjoining room and returned holding an address book.

"Here you are. The address of her flat in Manchester. Before she became ill she got a job with a modelling agency there."

"Thank you, Mrs Baxter, you've been very helpful."

* * *

They made their way across the police station car park. Lily yawned. "I'm knackered."

Matt smiled. "Did you notice? She referred to the courthouse in Huddersfield. Anita was doing law, and spent time in the public gallery, and Caroline had done jury service there."

Lily stood still for a moment, putting it all together. "Robert Nolan is a solicitor. He will work there and elsewhere. He could have seen Bella in the past and not let on."

"We can't ignore it. We'll see what Carlisle's come up with, then we'll call it a day. We'll look into the link with the courthouse tomorrow."

When they reached the incident room, Beckwith was updating the incident board. "You were right. Seems both Crosland and Firth knew Caroline Sheldon. The super wants another briefing before we finish."

Lily groaned.

"Got somewhere to go?" Matt asked her.

Lily stepped back in mock surprise. "You mean do I have a life away from the station? On a Thursday night I do, as it happens. I'm a member of the pub darts team. We're practising for a big match that's coming up."

"Any good?"

"We pass, with the odd stroke of brilliance. A bloke called Greg's our star player. When he's in the mood, that is."

Matt smiled. "I might pop down and watch you sometime."

"Please don't, that'd put me right off. It's bad enough with Greg making stupid comments all the time. Reckons I can't throw for toffee. But I made the team, so I can't be that bad."

"He's probably jealous. Take no notice. Is Greg the team captain?"

"Yes, and in case you're wondering, he's also my fella."

Matt smiled to himself. He hadn't noticed a ring on Lily's finger, and he hadn't asked. Relationships were notoriously hard once you had on that detective's hat. The job left little time for anything else. Still, with her having no parents, it was good that she had someone in her life.

"You got anyone, sir?"

He smiled again. "Apart from my mother, you mean?"

Lily clapped her hand over her mouth in mock regret. "Sorry, shouldn't have asked. Too bloody nosy, that's my problem."

"It's okay, and the answer is no. There is no one. Hasn't been for a while."

Dyson's voice boomed out. "Alright you lot! Let's get this over with."

The team gathered in the main office in front of the board. Carlisle kept glancing at the office clock on the wall. He looked annoyed. No doubt he wanted this to be over quick so he could get off. Beckwith, on the other hand, had his eyes fastened on some paperwork. He looked more engrossed than he had in days. Perhaps he had the makings of a good detective after all.

"DI Brindle. What have you got?"

"We're following a lead given to us by the mother of Deborah Thornley, sir. Our unknown victim could be Anita Verity, one time model, lately turned recluse due to mental health issues. We also have a link with Huddersfield courthouse, but it needs further investigation. It is possible that the killer identified his special victims there."

"Good. Have you spoken to the Richards boy yet?"

"No. He was sleeping when we went. I'll do that tomorrow. His mother said the lad had been rambling about the man with tattoos. About that — our killer could be using the tattooed arms thing to deliberately mislead us. Caroline Sheldon's boss reckons the man she was seeing had none. Which doesn't tally with what Oliver or the lad in the newsagents said."

"DI Carlisle, what do you have for us?"

Carlisle nodded to Beckwith, who stood up. "Sonia Crosland was a hairdresser. She worked in a salon in the centre of Huddersfield. According to her colleagues, she did know Caroline. The two had been friendly at school and met up after a gap of several years, shortly before Caroline was killed. They saw each other quite a lot. Caroline had her hair done at the salon regularly, and the two went out together. Prior to Caroline meeting this Doug bloke that DI Brindle found out about, the pair had gone speed dating at a pub in town."

"Do you know if she met Doug at one of these events?" Brindle asked.

Beckwith shrugged. "Her colleagues didn't know. Oscar Firth was a student at Huddersfield University. I spoke to a number of his friends, and none of them had heard of Caroline. However his tutor told me that Oscar did know her. He was doing up an old Mini Cooper for her in his spare time."

Dyson nodded. "Well done. We now know that all three green stamp victims knew Caroline Sheldon. No one has come forward to report her missing. No body has been found. So — the big question. Is she dead, or has she simply done one?"

"There was a false trail, sir," Matt reminded him. "The job in Glasgow that didn't exist. We will check out the Anita Verity angle in the morning. If she can't be found either, then we have to seriously consider that our killer has taken these women."

Dyson was silent for a moment, evidently considering this.

"If that is the case," Matt continued, "Then it's likely that Bella is in real danger. Considering what has happened recently to everyone close to her, I reckon that she is the killer's next target. We have a FLO keeping an eye out, but is that enough? Perhaps we should have her watched."

Dyson shook his head. "If Bella Richards is his third victim, it was a mistake on his part. Bella is subject to a layer of protection he knows nothing about. We can be assured that her contact will be keeping tabs on her. Apart from which she has spent most of her time at the hospital since her son was found. We have officers there."

"Is there a presence at her house, sir?" Beckwith asked.

Dyson looked at the team. "I don't think the killer will risk it. If she disappears, there will be an instant hue and cry. Our man has cocked up good and proper this time. Also Bella has attracted attention because of the Chalker angle. She is now well-known and has people around her. No more living the quiet life for Ms Richards."

"We should ensure her safety ourselves, sir," Matt told him. "The witness protection crew are good, but we don't want any mishaps, do we? If there isn't anyone there currently, then we should get it arranged."

Dyson nodded at Matt. "Ring the woman and tell her. Tell her to stay put until one of our people gets there."

Chapter 30

It had been a long day. Matt was tired, but buoyed by the fact that they were making progress. It was dark when he left the station. He was about to hop into his car when a woman called out to him from the shadows. "Hello, you!"

He swung round. The voice had soft, rounded tones, with a hint of huskiness. He'd know it anywhere.

"Melissa!"

"You didn't ring, there were no texts. I've given you long enough, Brindle. So here I am."

She stepped into the light. Her blonde hair was pulled into a ponytail. She was wearing a loose, well-worn waxed jacket over jeans and a T-shirt. Her head was tilted to one side and there was just the hint of a smile hovering on her lips. She appeared to be unsure of her reception.

She stepped closer. "Come on, then. Do I get a hug or what?"

Matt didn't move. He was momentarily stunned. She was the last person he'd expected to see. It was over between them. He'd made himself clear enough six months ago. Had she not understood the words he'd written? "What are you doing here, Mel? Why didn't you call me first?"

"I've just told you — I did, on and off for weeks, and it got me nowhere."

"You shouldn't have come. You know what happened. I made it plain enough. I was a mess, both physically and psychologically. I didn't want you being part of that. Better to make a clean break."

He looked into those dark blue eyes and met her cool gaze. Matt always got the feeling she was sizing him up, and she could see right into him.

She shook her head. "Wasn't that my decision to make? Don't I even get a say? My opinion counts for nothing, does it? I thought we were in a relationship, that we loved each other. What did you think I'd do, Matt? Did you think our relationship was so shaky that I'd do one after you were hurt? There's no way I'd have done that. I would have helped you recover."

Matt spread his hands. "You would have felt obligated. I didn't want that. Anyway, I was a terrible patient. I left the nursing to my mother. Despite all the airs and graces, she's a tough old bird, and could take the flack."

She laughed. "I'd like to have seen that!"

"Tone it down, Mel. I owe my mother a lot. Without her, I doubt I'd have made it. Have you been round to the house?"

"Didn't see the point. Your mother was unlikely to give me the time of day. You remember how it was. I was nothing but an irritation. I certainly wasn't lady of the manor material." She looked away, shaking her head. "I read about the case you're working on in the paper, and decided I stood a better chance of finding you here."

There was a time when Melissa Gibbs had been the love of his life. Had things been different, he would have married her. The incident, and not his mother, had put paid to that. That decision had hurt him almost as much as the grenade had.

"You can do better than me, Mel. I'm no good for anyone, not anymore. I've changed. I can do my job, but—"

Melissa faced him, her hands on her hips. "That bloody job! Return to work, give your all to being a damn good detective, but sod what we had!"

"I'm doing you a favour."

"No, you're not. You are taking the easy way out. I thought you were better than that, Matt Brindle. All those weeks of lying on your back, helpless. Your mother got to you, didn't she? Kept on and on about how I was no good for you. How I'd bring down the Brindle name if you got too involved!"

"No! What I did was entirely down to me. Selfish as it might appear, it was the only way. I'm not better yet. I can live with how I am, but I can't expect you or anyone else to do the same."

"And your mother?"

"She bought in for the duration when she gave birth to me." Matt gave her a sad little smile and opened the car door.

"Are you seeing someone else?"

"No. It's pointless. Leave it, Mel. You're better off without me."

"We will see each other. You can't avoid it, I'm afraid."

"Why? What have you done?"

"I got fed up with living in London so I decided to come home. The team at Huddersfield had a vacancy for a social worker. I applied and got the job. So here I am." She smiled at him, and those big blue eyes shone with defiance. "Until I know the ropes, I'm working with the Emergency Duty Team."

Chapter 31

Day 16

Bella felt dizzy and faint. She had no idea what had happened, just a vague recollection of someone talking to her — then nothing. She couldn't even remember who that was. She regained consciousness half-sitting in a dark, cramped space. Panic took hold as she struggled to make sense of her surroundings. She couldn't extend her legs properly or move her arms. Both her ankles and wrists were tied tight, and her mouth was gagged. Her wrists had been tied behind her back, but with a bit of manoeuvring, she was able to run her fingers over the wall to one side of her. It was hard, like plasterwork. Underneath her was wood, possibly floorboards. Where was she, and how long had she been here? Fear and adrenalin sharpened her senses. She tried desperately to prise open the rope binding her wrists. But there was no way she could escape without help. The realisation struck her like a sharp blow to the guts. Whoever had taken her had rendered her helpless, and locked her in a cupboard.

Bella tried to scream, but the gag was too tight, and nothing more than a muffled whimper emerged. Squirming around in the dark, she hit her head on something hard. Raising her right knee slightly, she was able to kick out with her foot. Anyone close would hear the sound. She groaned. Stupid! No one would come. He'd have taken her somewhere no one would find her. Bile rose in Bella's throat, almost choking her. Finally they had won. This was the end.

* * *

Matt rang Lily and suggested they meet up at the hospital. They'd talk to Oliver Richards, and then continue the search for Anita Verity. They had the address of her flat in Manchester, so that's where they'd look first.

Lily was waiting for him when he arrived at Oliver's room. "Bella isn't here. It's a problem because Oliver can be discharged this morning. That solicitor, Nolan, arrived about ten minutes ago. He's been round to her house, and she isn't there either. Apparently they'd arranged last night that he would pick her up this morning, bring her here, then he'd take her and the boy home."

"I spoke to her last night, and told her about the officer we were sending. She promised to stay in until he arrived."

"I presume Beckwith organised that one, but I've heard nothing.

"Was Alison Wray at the house?" Matt was beginning to feel uneasy.

"Nolan said she wasn't, and to make sure, I rang her mobile. Alison didn't stay over last night. She's doing daytime only now. The last time she saw Bella was yesterday afternoon."

Matt took out his phone and rang Bella himself. No answer. "If she doesn't turn up soon, we could have a problem. Where is Nolan?"

"He's minding Oliver."

Matt rang Beckwith next. "You did arrange for someone to watch over Bella last night? Only we can't find her."

"Uniform were getting it sorted," he replied. "Someone should have been there within an hour of us discussing it."

It looked very much like something had gone wrong. "Find out who was on duty and if they saw her. Get back to me urgently on this one."

They went into the room. Oliver Richards was sitting on the bed, dressed and with his bag packed. Nolan was talking to the nurse.

Matt smiled at him. "Hello, Oliver. Can we have a chat while we wait for your mum to get here?"

Nolan held up a hand. "Perhaps we should give it a little while longer. His mother should really be present."

"You're Bella's solicitor, why don't you stand in for her?" Matt suggested. "I'm only going to ask the lad about that day."

Oliver started to look interested. "Are you a policeman?"

Matt nodded. "Yes, but you are not in any trouble. It's that nasty man we want to catch."

"He wasn't nasty to me. He wanted to give me some comics." Oliver lowered his eyes. "I shouldn't have got into his car though. Mummy says I mustn't do that again. But he seemed okay."

"Do you remember where he took you?"

"No. I think I fell asleep."

Matt looked at Lily.

"Did he give you a drink, Oliver?" she asked.

"Yes, some cola I think. After that I don't remember much. I woke up in a dark room. The lady who was there wasn't nice. The room was cold too, and she didn't give me much to eat. The other lady was a lot kinder."

"Can you remember anything else about the man?" asked Lily.

"He had big tattoos on his arms. One was a dragon. I told him that I'm getting one too when I'm bigger."

Matt smiled. "Thanks, Oliver. If you think of anything else and want to talk to us, tell your mum."

Nolan checked his watch. "Bella must be running late. She obviously misunderstood last night when I said I'd pick her up. I'm not surprised. She was very tired."

"If she turns up or contacts you, let me know at once," Matt told Nolan.

Out in the corridor, Matt rang the station and brought DC Beckwith up to speed. They had to treat Bella's no-show as serious. "What happened last night?"

"A couple of PC's in a squad car were given the job. They did speak to her early on, just after tea-time. But a little later they got an emergency call from the pub around the corner. A bloke was trying to rob the place. He was wielding a baseball bat at the punters. Our crew were the nearest and had no choice but to attend. As it was we've got two life threatening injuries and a broken arm."

"This morning Bella is not where she should be. Get round to that house. Ask the neighbours, knock on doors and find out when they last saw her. It's possible she got the bus or a taxi to the hospital. If she did, Bella would have waited for it on the High Street. Ask the shopkeepers if they saw her. Let me know what you find."

"You're worried, aren't you, sir?"

"Yes, Lily. Bella knew Oliver would be discharged this morning. There's no way she wouldn't come for that."

"The tat thing — first he has them, then he doesn't. He's playing us, isn't he?"

"Possibly in more ways than one."

"Are we still off into Manchester?"

"Yes. Despite all this, we still need to know what happened to Anita Verity."

* * *

As usual, the traffic on the M62 was heavy. After miles of tailbacks they eventually made it onto the Mancunian Way dual carriageway and into the suburb of Hulme.

Lily looked around. "It's not where you'd expect to find a top model. It's all tower blocks and concrete."

"A model down on her luck and hiding away. It's not too bad. There's a lot of regeneration going on. The skyline towards the city centre is looking good. Where is this block? According to the sat nav, we've arrived."

They were in a large parking area right in the centre of a semi-circle of tower blocks.

Lily pointed. "Crosby House. That's the one. Anita lived at number eighty. What's the betting it's all the way up there?"

They turned their eyes skywards. "If we don't find her, we'll see what the neighbours know."

The block had recently been refurbished, so the lift was working. Plus all the paintwork was spic and span, and there were flower boxes on several of the windowsills.

"Looks lived in anyway." Matt pressed the doorbell of number eighty.

But the woman who answered was definitely not Anita Verity. She was Asian and elderly.

"I am DI Brindle and this is DC Haines. We're from the East Pennine police. We are looking for this woman." Matt and Lily showed the woman their badges, and then Lily showed her the photo.

The woman shook her head. "I do not know this person."

"Have you lived here for long?"

"Two years. The flat had been empty for a while, so I was told. It was done up and then I moved in. My neighbour who lives along there, number eighty-six, she has been in this block for years. She may know the woman. Why don't you ask her? As a rule she knows everything that is going on around here."

Matt thanked her and they walked along the corridor. "Keep your fingers crossed."

He banged on the door.

The woman's name was Gail Prosser. She appeared to be quite happy to talk. "You know, I said at the time that it wasn't normal. He was a funny bugger too. Calling at all times of the day and night. And the noise! Played his music loud enough to wake the dead."

"And this was a friend of Anita's?"

"Love of her life, so he said. Mind you, Anita didn't say much to back that up. I got the impression that he had some sort of hold over her."

Matt and Lily exchanged glances. "Did he boss her about? Stop her going out, seeing her mates, how did this 'hold' show itself?" Lily asked.

"He certainly didn't like her talking to folk. Always butted in if he found us chatting on the corridor. He'd take hold of her hand and drag her off, forcibly too."

"When was the last time you saw her?" Lily asked.

"Well, that's the funny thing. I didn't even realise she'd gone. It went a lot quieter, but I didn't think anything of it. It was Christmastime, I remember. I popped round with a card and got no answer. I gave it until the New Year, then I called again. I looked through the letter box and could see the mail stacking up. I didn't think she'd be on holiday. Rarely went to the corner of the street, did Anita. Lived on her nerves, you know. In the end I rang the council. Someone came round and emptied the place. Said she'd done a moonlight flit. Not paid any rent for months."

"Have you heard anything from her? A phone call, a card? Or seen her out and about?" Matt asked.

"No. It's as if she's evaporated into thin air."

"Has anyone come looking, apart from us?"

"No, and that surprised me too. She has a cousin Huddersfield way. He used to come with his wife when she first moved in. But once she got with 'im that stopped too."

"Do you recall his name?"

"Doug something or other. I don't know if I ever heard his surname."

Lily took the image she had of the tattooed man from her pocket and showed the woman. "Is this him?"

"No! Nothing like. He had no tattoos for a start, and his hair was short. Quite good-looking though, I'll give him that. Mind you, Anita had been a model. Successful too, in her time."

They made their way back to the car.

"What do you think?" Lily asked.

"My gut tells me we're onto something. We can find no trace of Caroline or Anita. Neither of them had many people close to them. Both women are dead ringers for Bella Richards. The people we've spoken to about this 'Doug' all give similar descriptions. I think our killer has taken two of them, and is now making a play for Bella. She fits the specs perfectly."

Chapter 32

The traffic was still bad, so it took them the best part of an hour to get back to the station.

Dyson met them as they walked in. "We've got a problem. You left Beckwith investigating the whereabouts of Bella Richards. It would seem she's disappeared. Gone, and no one knows where."

Matt was worried that this was the case. "Our bloody watch was called to a job. Half an hour apparently, but that's all it took. Did he ask down the street, like I told him?"

Dyson nodded. "The lad did, and got nowhere. Although one of her neighbours said that colleague of hers was nosing around last night."

"Joel Dawson?"

"Yes. I've sent Carlisle to bring him in. It looks like he was the last person to see her. I've also got a forensics team going over the Richards home." Dyson shook his head. "You were right, Matt. I should have had her watched."

"What about her son?" Matt asked. "We left the boy in the hospital, ready to be discharged."

"The nurse is hanging onto him for a while. That solicitor is still there. He's asked for a word with you."

"Okay, we'll get down there. When Dawson is brought in, I wouldn't mind a word myself."

"Don't worry. He'll be staying for a while." Dyson walked away, shaking his head sadly.

Lily looked at Matt. "You think she's been taken, don't you?"

"It isn't looking good, is it? We need to map out in detail where Bella went and who she spoke to after yesterday afternoon."

"Joel Dawson? Odd sort, is he?"

"I met him at Fisher's funeral. He probably looks weirder than he is. He's keen on Bella though, and he shows it."

* * *

When the two detectives arrived at the hospital, Nolan was pacing up and down the corridor.

"Do you know what's going on? I haven't heard anything from Bella since last night. It's mid-afternoon now, and I'm worried. This isn't like her at all."

"We are investigating," said Matt. "Tell me exactly when you last spoke to her, and what about."

"I took her home at about five yesterday afternoon to freshen up. She was supposed to contact me when she wanted to return. I texted her at about six. She replied not to come round, that someone else was giving her a lift here."

"Did she say who?"

"No, but it's easy enough to work out. It'll be that Dawson chap. He was always hanging around, and Bella wasn't happy about it either. He made her nervous. His clingy ways bothered her."

"Do you have the text?" Matt asked.

Nolan scrolled through the texts on his phone and showed him. It was a short message. But right enough,

Bella confirmed she was fine, and that Robert had done enough for one day. Another friend, unnamed, was giving her a lift.

"What are you going to do about Oliver?" Robert asked.

"I will be taking care of him."

They all turned around to stare at the woman who had spoken. She came striding along the corridor towards them and showed them her ID.

"Melissa Gibbs, social worker, Huddersfield Emergency Duty Team. I'm here to ascertain the lad's needs and place him in temporary care."

Matt was stunned. He hadn't expected to see her again so soon, and certainly not in connection with his case. Melissa gave no indication that she knew him.

"I have found him a place with foster parents. They live in Marsden, so should his mother turn up, we can get this sorted quickly."

"Mel, I don't think you understand." Matt had unconsciously used her first name, and the others looked at him in surprise. "Oliver has been ill. He was kidnapped and kept from his mother for several days. He's traumatised, and will need special care. Not only that, he will have to be guarded night and day until this case is resolved."

"We know that. We have been fully briefed. But we have to act for the benefit of the child, and right now he needs to be out of here. He will be placed with caring people who will look after him."

Lily had been looking from one to the other. "He needs his mum."

"Well, she's not here, is she?" Mel replied.

Lily faced her. "We think she's been kidnapped too. She's in danger. She's not a bad parent. No way has Oliver been abandoned."

"I can't comment on her parenting skills." Mel's expression was stony. "Wasn't she under police protection, too?"

"Yes, but things went wrong. The upshot, Bella was taken. Can I speak to the boy?" Matt asked. "Ask if he's remembered anything else about the experience?"

"Not a good idea. He has enough on his plate right now. In a day or two, Matt, when he's settled in." Melissa handed Matt her card. "Keep me informed. When you find his mother, make sure you ring me straight away."

They stood and watched her march off towards Oliver's room. Lily nudged Matt. "Bloody social workers. Don't you just hate them? But I got the impression you knew her. Apart from being on first name terms, I could sense a 'thing' between you. I'm good at that."

Matt grinned ruefully. "I do know her, or rather I did. As for the 'thing' you're on about, that's all gone."

Lily smiled. "An ex. Wouldn't have thought she was your type."

"Mel has her work hat on today. She isn't usually so officious."

They had forgotten about Nolan. "I'll leave you to it," he said now. "Everything appears to be under control here. Let me know if you find out anything about Bella's whereabouts."

Lily was still watching Mel disappear. "She might talk like a social worker, but she doesn't look like one. Jeans and a hoodie? She's a bit too casual. And she has a tat on her wrist."

Matt smiled. "A heart. Nothing to do with me either. Something from years ago, before I even knew her."

They walked back along the corridor. Lily's phone buzzed. It was a text from Beckwith. Mary Mason had been taken ill during her interview with him and Carlisle. The paramedic who'd come to the station thought it was a heart attack. She showed it to Matt.

He groaned. "Great! Another bloody witness we can't talk to."

* * *

Bella opened her eyes. Had she been asleep, or unconscious? She struggled to remember. She'd been tied up in a small space, but now her limbs were free, and the gag gone. A beam of sunlight filtered through a half-open door. She blinked. Was it real, or part of some drug induced dream? She could see outside! There was nothing stopping her making a run for it. Bella turned her head and realised she was lying on a bench, covered in a blanket. Her head was still fuzzy. Would she be able to stand?

Bella raised herself up on her elbows. She was in a windowless room, cold and dark apart from the strip of light shining through the doorway. But more importantly, there didn't appear to be anyone about. Bella pulled off the blanket and slipped off the bench. She put her feet on the ground and realised she was barefoot. Her limbs ached and so did her head, but she had to try. She inched towards freedom, hardly daring to breathe.

"No, you don't, my lovely."

She recognised that voice. It belonged to a man she trusted. Bella spun round. For one glorious moment, she thought he'd come to rescue her. But then she looked into his face. It was gloating. He was seated in an armchair, half-hidden in the shadows. Had he been there all the time, watching her? Bella stared back, horrified. How could she have been so taken in by this man?

She found her voice, and screamed at him. "You! I don't understand. Why are you doing this? You can't keep me here. I need to go. I have a sick child, and you know it!"

He was leaning back in the armchair, quite calm, quite matter of fact. "Calm down, Bella. It isn't good for you to get angry. If you behave, I'll give you something to eat. I'll let you come into the house."

"It was you all the time, wasn't it? You did all those dreadful things. You are the one who made my life hell!" She swayed on her feet, and her head span. This was beyond awful.

He laughed. "I had no choice. They were in my way, all of them."

"You killed Alan. You took Olly from me. My child could have died." She looked at him in disgust. "You are a monster!"

"No, I'm not. I am a man who loves you. And you will love me back."

Bella shook her head vehemently. "Never! Go to hell! I want nothing to do with you. You will not get away with this. People will come. The police will be looking for me."

He shook his head and tutted, as if she were a naughty child. "You are wrong. I will get away with it. Think about it. The police know nothing. What exactly have they got? How are they going to find me?"

"They are clever, especially that Brindle. He will know what to do."

"You are fooling yourself. I can do what I want, and no one will stop me. And as for you, Bella, either you love me — or you die."

Chapter 33

Day 17

"You're not going to like this." When Matt came in the next morning, Dyson was waiting for him. "We've had a request from Ron Chalker's solicitor. Chalker has asked to see you."

That threw Matt completely. "Why would he want to see me? What does he imagine I can do for him? How has Chalker even got hold of my name?"

"God knows. You weren't named in the newspaper article. Bloody prison. Information runs through there like water through a sieve. Unless Bella said something to him."

"Do you think I should go?"

"Give it some thought. Don't rush into anything. After all, Chalker's not going anywhere." The super paused. "Something else. We can't find Dawson. He appears to have done one. Carlisle had to break into his house. Everything was okay, there was no sign of a struggle. They searched the place and they couldn't find his passport. We've issued alerts and a description."

Lily was frowning. "Why would Joel Dawson run, sir?"

"He must have got wind that we're looking for him. He could be our man — our Mr Apology. What do you think?" The super looked at both of them.

"Nolan thought that he was watching Bella. He said she was wary of him," Matt said.

Lily shook her head. "So why didn't she say? Honestly, you'd think folk would get it. People have been killed, women have been taken, never to be seen again, and she sits on something like that."

Matt smiled at her. "He'll be picked up soon enough. If it is him, we'll know. We have DNA taken from Agnes Harvey that came from the killer."

"If he has run, what about Bella? What's he done with her? Taken her with him?" Lily looked at him.

"That's what's worrying me."

"Me too," said the super, and walked away.

"Not the only thing either, I would imagine." Lily said, once the super was out of earshot. "I heard the bit about Chalker. Scary, if you ask me. The man's a killer, and he's clever. If you go, you'll have to watch your step."

"I'm just intrigued to know what he wants. But we can't ignore him. He might know something about Bella's disappearance."

Lily pulled a face. "Then again, he could be plotting something. He'll know about her disappearance anyway, sir. It's been on the telly, last night's local news."

Matt rolled his eyes. "I thought we were keeping things quiet."

"Don't look at me. They got the story from someone, but it didn't come from here."

Matt looked thoughtful. "It's possible that our killer leaked the information."

"Why would he do that, sir?"

"I don't know, but he'll have some twisted reason."

Matt had a pile of paperwork on his desk but he couldn't concentrate. The days were passing, and things were just getting worse. Apart from finding Oliver, they were nowhere. Now they'd lost Bella, and Joel Dawson was missing. They desperately needed a break.

Lily looked up from her desk. "Did we check out that 'Doug' person? I've just spotted his name circled in my notebook."

Matt was slow to reply. Lily had given him an idea. "Both Caroline and Anita had a new boyfriend called Doug. I know we decided that wasn't his real name, but the man himself was real enough. So who was he?"

"A man who'd come into their lives just before they disappeared," Lily replied. "Someone with no distinguishing features, but who we think likes to disguise himself as the 'tattoo man.'"

"So what about Bella? Who is her 'Doug?'" Matt asked, almost to himself.

"We haven't seen Bella with anyone like that. She was in love with Fisher. She wouldn't have wanted anyone else in her life just yet. And Fisher's dead, sir, so he's not the killer."

"Bella led such an insular life that there aren't many men to choose from. But Joel Dawson is one of them. She's known him for two years, and works with him. If he is our killer, why would he choose now to strike?"

Lily shrugged. "Because he could? An opportunity presented itself?"

"I don't think so, Lily. He'd have been better striking before she got involved with Fisher. That affair had only been going on for a few months."

"If not Dawson, then who? There isn't anyone else."

Matt smiled. "Yes there is. You're forgetting Robert Nolan."

"The solicitor? You really suspect him?" Lily asked.

"Think about it. Caroline and Anita both had occasion to visit Huddersfield courthouse. They could have met Nolan there. I reckon it would do no harm to look a little deeper at our Mr Nolan, and his life. Like Dawson, he is always around, sticking his nose in. We could start by talking to Anna Fisher, Alan's widow. Nolan is her neighbour."

DC Ian Beckwith almost ran into the incident room. "Forensics have found blood on the carpet in the sitting room of Bella's house! Also a discarded cigarette end in the porch outside There's an overturned coffee table and crockery scattered all over the place. All the signs of a struggle."

"Did you ask the neighbours if they heard anything?" asked Matt.

"I asked if they'd seen Bella yesterday. The woman next door, the one who let the kid slip through her fingers, recalls hearing shouting at about seven last night. Reckons she heard a car drive off."

"Did she see it?"

"No. It was dark and her curtains were drawn."

"Okay. Jot it down on the board. It might prove useful."

"There is something else. We found her second mobile. It was hidden in the greenhouse. I had a quick look before forensics took it away. There were only two contacts. One was the dead woman, Agnes Harvey — she was listed as 'Auntie.' The other was simply listed as 'James.' Here's the number." Beckwith handed Matt a piece of paper.

Matt smiled at the DC. "Good work. We should have a word."

Lily looked up from her computer. "What are you thinking?"

"This is probably her contact from witness protection. That day she went into Manchester, I think she went to meet him. She had the phone with her then. He may not be aware of what's happened."

"That's a bit of a leap. This 'James' could be anyone."

"No, Lily. He's someone Bella had to keep secret. I will ring him and find out."

"Where does Anna Fisher live, sir?" asked Lily.

"Back of Marsden. That new housing development near the reservoir."

"The one they call 'Millionaire's Heights?'"

"Yes, that's the one. It's a big house, with plenty of land around it. I've been there, remember? Fisher's funeral."

"You've met his wife?"

"No. Oddly enough, I didn't. Anna Fisher wasn't there. I didn't give it much thought at the time, but now I'd like to know why."

* * *

Lily was looking up at the Fisher house. "What d'you reckon these go for, sir? I remember them being built, about ten years ago. Caused a right stink. This area is supposed to be green-belt land."

"Come on, let's get this done." Matt had no idea what to expect from the visit — or Anna Fisher. She had not attended the funeral. Why, since she'd never divorced her husband?

"She isn't here!"

An elderly man appeared through a side gate carrying a garden spade. "I've not seen Mrs Fisher for several weeks. She never said anything to me about going away, and the house is all shut up."

"Do you have a key?"

The man shook his head. "Only to this gate and the shed. I come every fortnight to help in the garden."

"Do you remember exactly when you last saw her?" Matt asked.

"The day before her husband was killed. She rang and asked me about some begonias for the summer display. I brought some round for the greenhouse that afternoon."

"Did she seem okay?" asked Lily.

"Right as ninepence."

"Do you know Robert Nolan, the solicitor who lives next door?"

The man nodded. "Nolan? Big bloke. Lawyer. I don't know him, but he and the Fishers were friends."

So Nolan checked out. Matt couldn't make up his mind if he was pleased about this. "Do you know anyone who might know where Mrs Fisher has gone?"

"She has a sister in Cornwall — Carol Sykes. Mrs Sykes and her husband have a pub in Truro, the Bull Inn."

Chapter 34

Once they got back to the station, Matt called a short briefing. He wanted the team brought up to speed with what they'd got. The news wasn't good.

"Joel Dawson?" Matt asked.

Beckwith shrugged. "No trace. He's disappeared off the face of the earth. I've asked his neighbours, the college. I even had a word with the group of students he's course tutor for. Nothing."

"It is possible that Anna Fisher has also disappeared. Of course, she may have gone on holiday, but we can't presume that. The gardener hasn't seen her since the day before her husband was killed. But we have got a lead. A sister in Cornwall." He handed Beckwith the name and address. "Check it out as soon as you can. If she's there, I'd like to speak to her myself."

"Is she important?" Carlisle asked.

"Truth is, I don't know. But Anna Fisher wasn't at her husband's funeral. We need to find her. She may know something. She may even have been threatened herself."

"The blood found at Bella's house was hers," Beckwith confirmed. "So she's been injured. But now the juicy bit. Saliva from the cigarette butt belongs to someone known to us. Tommy Johnson, a small-time villain who used to work for Chalker's firm."

"Chalker? Are you sure?"

Beckwith shook the paper at him. "Forensics are."

"Was there any sign of a break-in at her house?" Matt asked him.

Beckwith shook his head. "No."

"Bella is unlikely to know someone like Johnson. A lone cigarette end means nothing. I still think Bella knew her attacker. She would not open the door to just anyone. She is well aware of the danger she's in." Matt sighed. "So that leaves us with Dawson or Nolan."

"We can't ignore the evidence. Was anything else found?" the super asked Beckwith. "Fingerprints for example?"

"No, just the fag end."

Carlisle nodded. "Well, if we are going with her knowing him, my money's on Dawson."

"Don't be so quick to judge," Matt said. "We should look closer at Nolan. We know very little about the man. His address checks out and he *is* a solicitor, but we need meat on the bones. A detailed account of what he's been doing during the past twenty-four hours will do for a start." He turned to Lily. "Find out where he is today. We need to see him."

"And what task are you getting on with, Brindle?" Carlisle sneered.

Matt smiled. "I'm going to speak to someone from witness protection."

The incident room was a hive of activity. Matt sat at his desk and pressed the number for 'James,' from Bella's second mobile phone.

"Hello." The voice was clipped and business-like.

"This is DI Brindle, East Pennine CID. I believe that you are Bella's contact in the witness protection team."

There was a silence.

Finally, 'James' spoke. "You should not ring this number. It is for emergencies only."

"This is an emergency," Matt said. "Who am I talking to?"

"The phone you are using — where did you get it?"

"We found it at Bella's house, but that isn't important. You may not be aware of this, but she is missing. There are signs of an altercation at her house, and she has disappeared. We strongly believe that she has been kidnapped."

Matt waited.

"I am aware of the case you are investigating. How much do you know about Bella's past?"

"Enough. I know she is on the protected persons programme, because of the threat from her ex-husband, Ron Chalker. And I am guessing that you are her contact."

Matt heard a sigh.

"I told Bella it was a mistake to visit Chalker. She insisted that he would learn nothing from her, but you will have seen the papers. He would have been able to find out her location. I did warn her. I urged her to move again, but she refused, said her son was too poorly."

"I am trying to ascertain if Bella's disappearance is to do with her ex-husband, or a case we're investigating."

"I have nothing positive to offer, sorry. But if I had to go with one or the other, I would choose Chalker. He has seen his chance and grabbed it. The man still has influence, there are people he can call on to do his bidding."

"You should know also that Ronnie Chalker has requested a visit from me."

"Be very careful. He is a villain and an accomplished liar. Do not take anything he tells you at face value. There will be an ulterior motive behind everything he discusses with you."

"Given the man's reputation, I would like to be able to rule Chalker in or out. Look, I realise that it is in the nature of your work to operate with a high degree of secrecy, but Bella is in danger. She has already told me she is in the programme. Are you aware of a definite threat from Chalker?"

"You will have to make up your own mind on that one once you've spoken with him."

"You still haven't told me your name. I may need to contact you again."

"You do not need to know who I am. If you want to speak to me, ring the same number. Best of luck. I hope you find her. Keep me informed of progress." He ended the call.

Lily was watching him. "You don't look happy."

"He wasn't any help. He had no real information to offer. What about Nolan? Any progress?"

She smiled. "I looked him up. He's a partner in a firm in Halifax, called Bradfield and Nolan. I rang, and got the receptionist. She said he is scheduled to appear in court in Huddersfield this afternoon, and may be back in the office later."

Matt was beginning to think they would never get anywhere.

"Mobile?"

Lily nodded. "I tried it, but it's turned off. I could nip into town and find him."

"Do that, would you, Lily? Ask him to come in and see me."

Beckwith knocked on the office door. "Anna Fisher. I've found her. Here is her mobile number, and she's happy to speak to you."

Matt dialled the number. Anna Fisher answered immediately.

Matt introduced himself. "I have a couple of questions. The first is a little personal, I'm afraid. Can you tell me why you didn't attend Alan's funeral?"

"I went to the service, DI Brindle. I arrived late and sat at the back. I doubt anyone will have noticed me. I left before the end. I had my bags packed in the car, and went to my sister's straight away. I couldn't face the wake, or the weeks to follow. Alan and I had had our problems, but things were still reasonably okay between us. In my own way, I still loved him. We shared a lot of history. And I knew that Bella Richards would be there. She must be devastated. I feel for her, but there's nothing I can do to help. I simply wanted to be out of the way."

"Did you notice anyone hanging around your house before Alan was killed? In fact, anything odd at all in those last few days?"

"No. Everything was as usual. No strangers, no funny phone calls."

"And Alan never voiced any fears about being followed or watched?"

"No, but I doubt he'd have told me anyway. If Alan were to confide about something like that to anyone, it would have been Robert, our neighbour."

"Yes, I've met him. Thank you, Mrs Fisher, you have been very helpful."

DC Beckwith called out excitedly. "We've got Dawson! Traffic have just chased him up the M60. He came unstuck at the pyramid junction, hit a barrier and narrowly missed being trashed. He's in Manchester Royal with concussion."

Matt checked the clock. It was the rush hour, and the traffic would be horrendous. "Can he talk?"

"He's in Resus under guard. The nurse reckons he's in no fit state tonight. Doesn't even know his own name. She says tomorrow at the soonest."

"Was he alone in the car?"

Beckwith nodded. "It's being towed into forensics as we speak."

If Dawson had taken Bella, what had he done with her? Matt was tired and couldn't think straight. He should really go home. His leg was aching so much that he could barely get up from his chair. He was about to go down to the canteen and get something to eat when his phone rang.

It was Lily. "No one at the court has seen Nolan today, sir. Proceedings had to be cancelled. He hasn't rung in or anything. They are as mystified as we are. Apparently he's never done this before. If it's alright with you, I'm going home. It's taken an age just to get here. Finding a parking spot was a bugger too."

Matt had a bad feeling about this. First Joel Dawson had disappeared, and now it was Nolan's turn. What was going on? These were the only two men Bella Richards had had any dealings with recently. Was either of them Mr Apology?

Matt could see Dyson's bulky frame from his office. The super was standing in front of the incident board, staring at it.

Dyson tapped the board. "It's a bad do. Gone to ground, the bloody lot of 'em."

Matt hauled himself up and went to join him. "Not quite. We've caught up with Dawson now. Hopefully he'll talk to us tomorrow. We certainly need him to, because the truth is, Talbot, we haven't got a clue. We've exhausted all the leads, even the second mobile Bella had. She used it to ring her aunt and her contact on the programme. I rang him. Wouldn't even give his name. Big on sympathy but no help at all."

"We'll have to see what tomorrow brings. It's been a long day and like you, I'm knackered." He looked at Matt leaning heavily on the desk. "Why don't you get off home? That meeting with Chalker has been arranged for tomorrow afternoon at two. A uniform will drive you there."

Chapter 35

Day 18

Forensics had retrieved Joel Dawson's mobile phone after the car crash. On it were dozens of messages to Bella, plus numerous photos. Many more had been taken over the last couple of days. He had obviously been watching her closely. By the time Matt arrived at the station, everything found had been put on the system.

Lily was scrolling through a screenful of messages. "He kept texting her, but she rarely replied. Weird, if you ask me. Bella knew he was stalking her but she didn't complain to us."

"There are a stack of photos. It will take an age to go through them." Matt had them all up on his computer screen and was looking at them one by one. "Some go back weeks. There are even some of Bella and Fisher. This is incredible! The man must have spent most of his free time watching her. There is even one here of Bella pulling the curtains shut."

"If you ask me, Dawson's a major weirdo. D'you think she knew the extent of his obsession with her? If she'd said something to us, we might have put a stop to all this a lot sooner."

"Don't presume he's our man, Lily. Look at these."

Matt had scrolled on to the more recent images. "He must have taken some of these from his car, in front of the house."

"Not very good though, are they? That one shows Nolan leaving. It's date-stamped the night she went missing."

"Doesn't help, Lily. Nolan admitted to being there."

"Who is that?"

Lily pointed to another car parked a few metres down the street. Dawson had photographed a man sitting in the driver's seat. Matt shrugged. "He could be anyone. It's busy round there. Lots of houses, and parking is tight."

"No, look! Dawson's got him again, outside Bella's house."

The image wasn't bad. Dawson had caught the man's face illuminated in the street light.

Lily peered over his shoulder. "We've not seen him before. Late thirties or so, dark hair, smartly dressed. What d'you reckon he's up to?"

The next few images showed the man standing outside Bella's front door. In the final shot, she was letting him in.

"We need to know who this man is. But I know one thing, he isn't Tommy Johnson. It looks to me as if someone is trying to lay a false trail."

"You could be right. Johnson is linked to Chalker. Our killer is trying to lay the blame on him. Chalker has been all over the papers, and I'd say the killer has seen his chance and taken it. Mind you, we should ask ourselves where that cigarette butt came from." Lily looked back at the computer screen. "I'll lay odds that 'doorstep man' there is Doug. But if he is, where's he come from? He isn't in any of the other photos."

Matt attached the image to an email and sent it off to the tech boys to enhance. He would have to make sure there weren't any others. He looked through the photos again. There were dozens of them, some taken just days ago. A number of them had even been taken outside the prison in York. They showed Bella sitting in a car with a man. Bella was easy enough to make out, but the man was nothing but a blur. Matt kept looking. There was another. The same man, and the same car, taken on Huddersfield High Street. He looked at the date stamp — a couple of days before Chalker was all over the papers. Dawson had been thorough. Matt just wished he knew what it all meant.

Lily looked up from her phone. "The uniform watching Dawson has just texted me. He is conscious, and we can see him. It means a bit of a drive though."

Matt checked the time. "You go with Beckwith. Get a full statement — that is if he remembers anything. Take a copy of this photo with you, and see if he knows the bloke. But before you do that, would you visit Riley again, and show him this one?" Matt held up the image of the man on the doorstep. "Ask him if this is Caroline Sheldon's boyfriend, Doug."

"You, sir?"

Matt grimaced. "I've got a date with Ronnie Chalker a bit later. Don't want to be late."

* * *

Matt had no idea why Chalker wanted to see him. He presumed it must be something to do with Bella or their son. Whatever it was, he wasn't looking forward to it. Before being put away, Chalker had been heavily involved with organised crime. He was a cold-blooded killer. There would be an angle somewhere, it was just that Matt hadn't worked it out yet.

Matt spent the journey thinking through the case. Things were becoming clearer. Caroline, Anita and finally

Bella had all been to court for one reason or another. He suspected that the man Bella thought was her contact on the programme was not who he purported to be. But of course, he needed to prove that. He could only hope they would get the vital final pieces in time to save her.

Ronnie Chalker was sitting at a table. A guard stood in the corner of the room. It crossed Matt's mind that the villain wasn't a particularly beefy bloke. Should things get violent, the guard and he would probably have the upper hand.

Chalker had a grin on his face. "Found her yet?"

"No, but we will." Matt sat down at the table opposite and put a slim file in front of him.

"You'll be hoping the bitch is still in one piece. But I'll lay odds she's dead. Couldn't have worked out better if I'd planned it myself."

Matt knew the history, but he was still appalled. "Did you?"

The grin disappeared. Chalker's eyes narrowed as if he were trying to get the measure of him. "No, copper, I didn't. But I'm not sorry, not one bit. Izzie deserves a lot worse. Frankly it wouldn't bother me if she ended up dead in the cut."

"Izzie?"

"Isabelle — her real name. Calling herself Bella now, by all accounts. Thinks I don't know, thinks I know nowt." Chalker laughed. "Well, she's wrong. Problem is, if the bitch is dead, where will that leave our son? I'm not a fool. The boy is better off with his mum. That's the only thing that has kept her alive these last two years."

Matt looked at him. "That, and you not knowing where she is."

"I knew exactly where she was all the time. She's been alive because I wanted her to be. But one day, when the lad is grown up, I will get my own back."

"Do you know Tommy Johnson?"

"You know very well I do. He was one of my boys before I got banged up."

"We have evidence that puts him at Bella's house the night she disappeared. Do you have anything to say about that?"

Chalker raised his hands. "Nothing to do with me. If I wanted rid of the bitch, I'd get someone who'd do the job proper."

This was getting them nowhere. Matt was uneasy. All he wanted was for this to be over. "Why am I here?"

"I want a favour."

"Why should I help you?"

Chalker rose slightly off his chair and leaned forward. His face was only inches away from Matt's. His intense stare made Matt flinch. "Because I will help you in return."

"I don't want anything from you." Matt shuffled his chair back and folded his arms.

The grin was back. "Bad leg you've got there. Saw the limp as you walked in."

"That has nothing to do with you."

"No, but it has a lot to do with someone I know."

Matt's stomach turned over. The incident had been thoroughly investigated — not by him, he'd been too ill. An entire team had worked the case for weeks, but they'd never been able to make real headway. Whoever was responsible for his injuries and Paula's death was still out there.

"You see, copper, you crossed the wrong person. And that person wanted rid. You were too close to exposing something huge."

Matt shook his head. "We were unlucky. Small-time drug dealing, that's all it was."

"No, that's what it looked like. You were one lucky bastard to get out of that building alive. Luckier than your partner, that's for sure."

Matt looked away. Was Chalker winding him up? What happened that day had been all over the news. Chalker could have got the details from anywhere.

"What exactly do you know?"

Chalker put up his hand. "Not until you agree to help me."

"What is it you want?"

Chalker leaned forward again. "I want out of here. I want a move to Manchester — Strangeways."

"Why? What's the difference?"

"I'm not safe in here. I have enemies, and they've already tried to kill me once. One bastard threw me down the stairs. In Strangeways, I have mates who will look out for me."

"What you're asking is out of the question. I don't have the power."

"You know people, other coppers higher up the ladder. Speak to someone. Get it organised."

Matt knew he couldn't do anything to help him. "You are asking the wrong person."

"Well, you ask the right ones then. What I have to tell you is worth the effort."

"You will have to give me more to work with. I need something to take to my superiors. Tell me what we stumbled into. Why were we targeted that day?"

Chalker's grin became smug. "Does the name Jack Waddell ring any bells?"

Matt went cold. Chalker was bad enough, but Waddell was in a different league entirely. Waddell was the acknowledged head of organised crime in the north of England. The name was rarely spoken aloud, and that was because people — and that included some of his own colleagues — were terrified of him. Whoever got on the wrong side of Waddell would be lucky to get out alive. He was a villain of the old school, never got his hands dirty, which was why nothing had ever been proven against him. He made criminals such as Chalker look like small fry.

"You are saying that Waddell was behind what happened that day? That it was him who had my partner killed?"

"I'm saying nothing. Get me moved, and we'll talk proper. But know this, copper. It isn't just Waddell you'll be getting the lowdown on. He has friends in high places. One of them in particular is a high-ranking policeman. That's another reason the investigation into what happened that day went nowhere."

Chalker was taking a risk in talking so candidly to him, a policeman, and with a guard in earshot. Matt nodded towards the guard. "What about him?"

"He's okay. Knows to keep his mouth shut."

"I could report back to my super. Tell him what you've just told me."

"I'd deny it. And Stan there would back me up. He'd swear blind that all we talked about was Izzie and the boy."

This interview needed a change of direction. Matt flicked absently through the file. Inside were some questions he'd intended to ask about Bella and a photo of 'doorstep man.' He took the image out and showed it to Chalker. "Do you know this man?"

"Why?"

"Just answer the question. Have you ever seen him before?"

Chalker shrugged. "Might have. Like I said, get me moved and I'll talk to you."

"It is imperative that we find him." Matt thought furiously. It was no good appealing to Chalker on behalf of Bella, better if he tried Oliver. "This is the man who took your son. He wasn't kind. He didn't take care of him. He made Oliver ill. He would have killed him too, if we hadn't found the boy in time. Surely you want him caught and dealt with?"

Matt watched Chalker wrestle with this.

"Bloke's an idiot. He used to write to me, asking all sorts of rubbish stuff. Wanted to know about me and Izzie before I got banged up."

"Did you write back?"

"What d'you think? Course I didn't."

"Have you ever met him?"

"He's some sort of clerk at the solicitors who took my case. He was with my solicitor a couple of times during the trial."

"Do you know anything else about him? His name? Where he lives? Was it on the letters?"

Chalker shook his head. "Nope. He didn't want a reply in writing. He wanted a visiting order. If I agreed, I was to arrange things through my solicitor."

"Who was your solicitor?"

"I used a firm in Halifax. Bradfield and Nolan."

Matt stared at Chalker. This was a link he hadn't reckoned with. But what did it mean? "Which partner dealt with you?"

"Bradfield. Wasn't the other one's area."

"Did you keep any of the letters?"

"No, I binned them. I've no interest in writing to some weirdo. What d'you think I am?"

"What name did he use when he wrote to you?"

"Signed the letters as 'Doug.'"

Chapter 36

Matt went back to his car and sat for a while, breathing heavily.

His phone rang. It was Lily. "Dawson swears blind it wasn't him, sir. He reckons he's simply been watching Bella, trying to protect her from whoever. He saw 'doorstep man' that night, but he doesn't know him. He did a runner because he was scared. He knew what it looked like. He knew we'd go after him first."

"Chalker told me that 'doorstep man' is 'Doug.'"

Lily was silent for a minute. "How does a man like Chalker know that? He's banged up, for goodness sake! But he's right. I had a word with Riley, and he confirmed that the man in the photo — Doug, or 'doorstep man' — was Caroline's boyfriend."

"He wrote to Chalker in prison, asking about Bella. Chalker told me that Doug was a solicitor's clerk at Bradfield and Nolan in Halifax."

"That's Nolan's firm. This just gets better! Does this mean that Nolan knows 'doorstep man?' Are they in this together?"

"I have no idea, Lily. Is there any news on Nolan?"

"Nothing yet. He didn't return home last night. We had an officer on duty outside. If you ask me, he's got scared and run."

"I'm not so sure, Lily. Take Beckwith and a photo, and get round to their office in Halifax. We need a name and an address for 'doorstep man.'"

"Didn't Chalker help with that?"

"No. He wants me to do something for him before he'll say anything more."

* * *

"You have been asleep, Bella."

"Where is this place?"

"You must not ask questions. It will be better for you if you accept that you are with me now, and I will look after you."

"I can look after myself. You have no right to do this."

Bella was no longer in the cold, dark room. She was lying on a sofa in a warm sitting room. A large antique grandfather clock stood in the corner, ticking away the seconds. The sound was driving her crazy.

He stood up and came towards her. "I have every right. You and I, we were meant to be together. I knew that the first time I set eyes on you, Bella. Don't you feel it too?"

He was mad, that was the only explanation. Bella was trying to recall what the police had told her. He was ruthless. He had killed others, not just Alan. Alan and Agnes had both been shot in the head. Bella was terrified. She was shaking badly and she thought she might vomit. She had to do something, try and keep him sweet until help arrived. She began to cry. "I don't feel well. My head aches. I banged it when I was tied up." She sat up, brushed her blonde hair off her face and tried a small smile. "Could I have a drink and some painkillers, please?"

"I will get you something."

He disappeared into an adjoining room. Bella looked around. The room was large, dominated by a huge fireplace. There were lacquered art nouveau cabinets, full of vases and figurines. All expensive stuff. This was evidently a man with money to spend on his individual taste. There were two doors leading off. The one he'd used probably led to a kitchen. But there was another, possibly leading out into a hallway. There was one window, but the blinds were pulled shut.

He was back with a glass of water and a couple of pills. "Take these."

Bella turned them over in her fingers to check that they were paracetamol.

"Take them. You will feel better."

She dabbed at her eyes. "Why have you brought me here?"

"Because we are meant to be together. You don't have to worry, Bella. You are quite safe with me."

Bella seriously doubted that. She had to escape, but knew it would be useless to try and fight. She needed to take a different approach. She must use every ounce of her self-control and stay calm, though what she really wanted to do was lash out and scream. "I'm worried about Olly. He will miss me. It will make him ill again."

"Your son is being well cared for. If you behave, I will bring you news of him. It's up to you, Bella, whether he stays fit and healthy. Do as I say, and all will be well. Don't let me down." He smiled. "I don't like hurting children."

Bella's blue eyes widened. Those words filled her with dread. He meant what he said. In all her dealings with this man, Bella had never had reason to doubt his integrity. She'd taken everything he'd told her, all he'd done for her, at face value. Had he meant any of it? Was he even who he said he was?

"Who are you?"

"You know who I am, Bella."

“No, who are you really? You aren’t who I thought you were, you aren’t—”

“Don’t! You will not use that name. From now on, you will call me ‘Darling’ at all times. Do you understand?”

Chapter 37

The moment the super entered the station, Matt made a beeline for him. "Can I have a word, Talbot?"

"That's a pensive look on your face. Chalker scared you half to death, did he?" Dyson clapped Matt on the back and led the way into his office. "What did he want? Say anything about that leak to the papers?"

"Not exactly. He wants my help." Matt closed the office door and sat down opposite Dyson. "He wants a move to Strangeways. He is offering certain information in return."

Dyson laughed. "That'll never happen. He's got too many cronies in that place. Within weeks, he'd be running the entire hellhole. Anyway, what could Chalker offer for a swap like that?"

"He told me he has information about that day. About who killed Paula and injured me."

"What can he know about that? Chalker was inside at the time. Besides, that was investigated. We did everything we could, but we came up against brick walls all the way. You know that." Talbot Dyson frowned.

"Yes, but why was that, Talbot? Why did you get nothing? If it was just a simple matter of dealing, finding the culprit should have been a doddle. Have you ever thought about that?"

"Course, I have. What happened was down to some backstreet drug dealer, out of his depth. Didn't want to get caught and went too far. He will have been an unknown. Went to ground, said nowt about it to anyone."

"Chalker says different. He told me that Jack Waddell was behind what happened that day."

The super blanched. He was silent for some time. "Knows that for sure, does he?"

Matt nodded. "Apparently I'd stumbled into something huge. Exactly what, he wouldn't say. But get him moved, and he'll be more forthcoming."

Dyson shook his head. "There is no chance of that."

"He did say more, but it's not good," Matt hesitated. Talbot wasn't going to like this. "Chalker said that Waddell was immune from investigation because he had a top copper on his payroll."

Dyson's face coloured up again. "The toe-rag is lying! No one in the force would give up the chance to get Waddell. Get Waddell banged to rights, and we'd sort half the crime in the north of England."

"Nonetheless, I'd like to look at the file again, sir. Perhaps I could take another look where I think it would be beneficial."

"Futile, lad. I know how you feel, how much you want to get the bastard who killed Paula. We all do, but Chalker is playing you. He's not stupid. He's picked on your one weakness, and he's using it for his own ends. Let it go, that's my advice."

There was a look on Dyson's face that Matt knew well. The super wanted the subject dropped, and there would be no persuading him.

* * *

Bradfield and Nolan Solicitors had their offices on the main route into Halifax centre. Beckwith was driving, and he pulled into the car park at the rear of the building.

"Got everything?" Beckwith asked Lily.

"All we need. A shedload of questions and a photo of 'doorstep man.'"

Lily and he walked round the building to the front entrance.

"How're you getting on with Brindle? Okay, is he?"

"He's really good to work with. No side to him at all. He's completely different to what I expected."

"He's some sort of posh twit, so I've heard. Public school."

Lily slapped his arm. "Don't be so rude, Ian. It was a private school on the outskirts of Leeds, nothing special. And he's no twit either. DI Brindle is a hardworking copper, just like the rest of us. That house he lives in doesn't reflect what he's like at all."

"Glad you're happy. Sounds as if you've fallen on your feet. I'm not so lucky. Carlisle's a dick. Spends as much time as he can on his backside. If I have to stay with him, I'm going nowhere, career wise."

"I'm hoping that DI Brindle stays with us. If he does, then I want on his team permanently."

"Sounds as if you've made up your mind, Lily. Put in a good word for me, will you?"

They entered the building and were shown into Guy Bradfield's office. Bradfield looked worried. His first words were, "Is this about Robert? It just isn't like him to disappear. We are all concerned. He was involved with that woman who was married to the villain, Chalker. A bad business that was."

Lily and Beckwith sat down, facing him.

"You acted for Ron Chalker," said Lily.

"I did, but make no mistake, there was never any chance he'd get off. The evidence was stacked high against him. These last couple of days have made me wonder if this isn't some sort of revenge."

Lily had no answer to that. As yet, the team did not know exactly how Nolan was involved in Bella's case. "It was you personally who acted for Chalker?" Bradfield nodded. "Was Mr Nolan involved at all?"

"No. In fact I don't think he ever met the man."

Lily handed him the photo of 'doorstep man.' "Do you know who this is?"

"Yes, it's Mark Turner. He used to work for us. Why? What is your interest in him?"

"He has been seen and photographed with Bella Richards recently. Bella is missing. We believe that this man uses the name 'Doug' on occasion, and that he may be responsible for the abduction of Bella, as well as her son, Oliver."

"But isn't the boy back now?"

Lily nodded. "Yes, but that was down to a tip-off and good detective work. So far we haven't been so lucky with Bella — or Nolan."

Bradfield shook his head. "Mark was a good bloke. Conscientious. He took his work seriously. I can't believe he'd be mixed up in anything of that sort."

"Do you know where he is now?"

"We will have his address on file. He left us just over two years ago, so I can't promise he'll still be there." Bradfield swung round on his office chair and peered into his computer screen. He printed out the address and handed it to Lily. "As you see, he lives on the outskirts of Shepley."

"Did Turner spend a lot of time in court?" Beckwith asked.

"Yes, all over — Leeds, Halifax and in Huddersfield. He also met a lot of unsavoury characters, Chalker among them. It was his job."

"Do you recall if he ever met Bella?" Lily asked.

"I can't say for sure. We were part of Chalker's defence team, and Bella was giving evidence for the prosecution. A lot of the sessions were done in camera. She was terrified of repercussions as I remember."

Lily stood up. "Thank you, Mr Bradfield. That's very helpful."

Bradfield opened the door for them. "Given the case you're working on, this is serious. I sincerely hope nothing has happened to Robert. The minute you find him, or if he contacts you, please let me know at once."

Chapter 38

Matt was writing notes on the incident board while he spoke. He had gathered the team for a review of progress. "We now know that Doug, our 'doorstep man,' used to work for Bradfield and Nolan, the solicitors who handled Chalker's case."

Matt caught Carlisle in the middle of a yawn. "Any news on Nolan?" he asked him.

Carlisle shrugged. "Nothing. Dropped out of sight. Bloke could be anywhere."

Matt frowned. "Not good enough. We need him found. Right. Dawson. Do we believe what he's told us?"

Carlisle shook his head. "He swears he's not involved, so your guess is as good as mine. Personally, I'd bring him in and beat the truth out of the bastard. He's as guilty as sin if you ask me. Look at the evidence, all those photos. There's the proof you need. He's been stalking the woman for weeks."

Carlisle's attitude was all wrong, but he had a point. "We must not forget that there are others in the frame. Nolan, for one. Until we know different, we'll treat his disappearance as suspicious. Also, Nolan's partner has identified Mark Turner as being the man we know as 'Doug.' He worked for their firm of solicitors up until two years ago. So what was he doing at Bella's house? How does he know her, and when did they meet? Was it during the Chalker trial? We must not forget that both Caroline Sheldon and Anita Verity had an interest in the law. Both women frequented the courtrooms." Matt looked at Carlisle. "We have found no evidence that Joel Dawson knew either Caroline or Anita. Given your prejudice against the man, perhaps you'd like to look at that again. In the meantime, Lily, Beckwith and I will take a ride out to Shepley. See if Turner still lives there."

Carlisle smirked. "Mob-handed,"

Matt spoke slowly, as if to a child. "He shoots people. If Turner is our man, he's dangerous." He tapped the board. "From what we've got, Turner is our likeliest candidate."

He could tell by the look on his face that Carlisle thought otherwise.

* * *

Lily drove them up the hill from New Mill towards Shepley village. "You think Turner saw Bella during Chalker's trial, and that's when he chose her as his next victim?"

"Yes, I do. But my theory has a flaw. Either of you spot it?" Matt turned to look at Beckwith, who sat behind him. He knew Lily was bright enough, but what about this young man? "Turner knows Bella from the time of the trial. He saw her at some stage. Lily, you said that Bella may or may not have been aware of him." Matt looked at Lily, then Beckwith. "Got it yet?"

Beckwith shrugged. "Seems straightforward enough to me. Turner could well be our man."

But Lily was thinking. "Bella has been in the protected persons programme. So how did Turner know where to find her?"

Beckwith poked at her back. "It's been in all the papers, div."

Lily shook her head. "No, you're wrong. We have photos of Turner watching her house *before* the news broke."

Matt nodded. "Exactly. That means Turner knew where Bella was. He has probably known all along."

"So who is he?"

"Who Bradfield told you he is — Mark Turner, former solicitor's clerk. But I suspect that he has been masquerading as Bella's contact in the protected persons programme. Despite what she believed, I doubt she was ever even in it. He could well have organised the move, her new identity, the lot, and kept up the pretence in order to isolate her."

"That is very clever. And it worked too. Until she fell for Fisher." Beckwith sounded impressed.

The address they had for Turner was a stone farmhouse clinging to the hillside about a mile from Shepley centre. It wasn't entirely on its own, however. There were houses within fifty metres or so, on either side.

Lily stared at the house. "It's a substantial property. Lots of rooms."

"It's had a lot of work done," Beckwith added. "The owner must have plenty of money."

Lily frowned. "The blinds are all shut. Whoever's living here obviously doesn't want snoopers, sir. How do you want to play this?"

Matt too was looking at the house. "Ring the station, Beckwith. Get some uniform up here. Get a photograph of Turner, and get it circulated urgently. There is no guarantee the man's at home."

"Your gut telling you something?" Lily asked.

"No, but the half-hidden red Ford Ka poking out of the shed on that path over there is," Matt said.

* * *

He had to sleep sometime, Bella was banking on it. But on the first night he locked her in a room on the top floor, with no way to escape. That morning she feigned sickness again, saying she had a headache and a sore throat. He gave her tea and tablets every four hours, but sooner or later he would see through her subterfuge.

"You've been so kind to me. I could help you," she suggested. "I can't lie on this sofa forever. I could tidy up, do a little cooking."

He smiled. "I'd like that, Bella. It'd make us more of a normal couple."

It killed her to do so, but she managed to smile back. It was vital to keep him sweet. If he lost his temper, God knows what he'd do to her.

"She is very pretty. A friend?" Bella had spotted a photo on the mantelpiece. It showed a blonde woman, of about her own age.

"That's Kitty. She was my wife."

Bella was surprised. He'd never said anything about having a wife, but then she'd never asked. "Where is she?"

He sighed. "Kitty was never satisfied. No matter what I did for her, it was never enough. I really tried, Bella. I did everything I could. I gave her every opportunity to do the right thing. But she drove me insane with her demands and her infidelities."

His voice had begun to rise. Talking about his wife was evidently winding him up.

"Did she leave you?"

"No woman leaves me, Bella." The words were hard, cold. They chilled her to the bone. "Once they come to this house, they are here for good. I like to keep all of them close."

"Have you brought others here?"

"Yes, Bella. Apart from Kitty, there have been two others. But they weren't right. They weren't a patch on you. Just like with Kitty, I tried everything, but they got it all wrong. They wanted things I could not give them. In the end I had to finish it."

What was he saying? Was he keeping them prisoner like her? Or had he killed them?

"That's sad. You haven't had much luck."

Her voice was shaking, and he was staring at her again. Had he seen through her? Did he know what she was doing, that she was just trying to keep him sweet? A shiver of fear flew down her spine and she felt genuinely sick. She wanted to ask more, but she didn't dare. If those women had been murdered, what had he done with the bodies? If she stood any chance at all of getting out of here, Bella had to convince him that she was different. She had to make him believe that she was on his side.

She smiled sweetly. "I do a mean cottage pie. If you buy the ingredients, I'll make it for dinner later. We could open a bottle of wine. Celebrate us getting together at last."

He leaned back and folded his arms. "I know what you're doing, Bella. In your position, no doubt I'd do the same. But be warned. I will not be taken in easily. You can smile and bat those pretty lashes all you want, but I don't trust you."

"That's a shame, because I'd like us to be friends. You have no idea how lonely it is on the program. Having to pretend to everyone you meet. Inventing stories about the past. It really is hard work. But you know all about me. I don't have to be anyone but myself with you. You know about Ronnie and what he did. You know what I have been through."

Mark Turner said nothing in reply, but took something from his pocket. It was the card from the bouquet of roses she'd left up on the moors. He waved it in her face. "I know all about Alan Fisher too. He was the only man for you. So what has changed, Bella? How can I trust someone who is so quick to forget the man she reckoned she loved so much?"

"I . . . I thought I loved Alan." Her voice faltered. "But I was infatuated with him. I was flattered that he liked me and got carried away." It killed her to say this. "What I really need is a man who understands what I've been through. Someone who I can be myself with. Someone like you, Mark." Bella waited, hardly daring to breath. He was watching her, weighing up what she'd told him. He had to be convinced, he just had to be.

"Why didn't you say something before? You could have rung, arranged more meetings. You had the phone I gave you."

"I didn't realise that you liked me then. But now that I know you better, I see that your way is best." She waited. His face was expressionless. He had to believe her. Bella could not keep up this pretence much longer.

Finally he smiled. "You don't have to cook if you don't want to. I don't mind if you take it easy, particularly if you're not well."

"Having something to do might help. It would take my mind off it."

"Okay, I'll go down to the village in a little while, and get some shopping. But I'll have to put you in that room again."

She made big eyes at him. "Please don't. I won't leave. You can trust me now, Mark. I'm quite enjoying my time here with you. You have a beautiful home. It's so peaceful and quiet. Life was so hectic where I was. Working took up all of my time. It's good to be able to wind down. This is the first time I've rested in weeks." Had she convinced him? Would he be taken in? She held her breath.

It worked. He smiled, and his whole face lit up. If he'd been a cat, he'd be purring right now. "Okay. I'll just lock the front and back doors. If you go into the kitchen, be careful of the floor. I'm laying a new one and it isn't quite finished yet. And don't go down into the cellar."

Chapter 39

Lily looked at Matt. They had moved further down the lane and parked in the driveway of the nearest neighbour.

"Are we waiting for backup to get here, sir?"

Before Matt could answer, Beckwith hissed, "He's leaving! Get down, or he'll see us."

The three detectives ducked.

After a few minutes, Lily sat up. "He was alone in that car. If she's in the house, now's our chance."

"Come on then, let's take a look."

They circled the building. There was one outbuilding, housing the Ford, but no others.

Beckwith hammered on the front door. "Anyone in there?"

"That's a heavy, old door." Matt gave it a shove with his shoulder but it didn't budge. "If we have to break in, it'll take some shifting."

Then they heard a woman's voice. "Hello?"

The three detectives looked at each other.

"Bella!" Matt shouted. "Are you okay?"

"You have to get me out fast. He won't be gone long."

Beckwith pushed open the letterbox so that he could see her. "We'll find a way in round the back. This door is too heavy."

Matt turned to Lily. "Stay here and keep an eye out for Turner. If he comes back, bang on the door."

He and Beckwith went round to the back of the farmhouse. There was a window they could use, but it was a fair way off the ground.

"I'll give you a leg up, then you knock out the glass with this." Matt handed Beckwith a large stone.

Beckwith slid through the window straight into the kitchen sink. He ran to the back door and after several hefty kicks, broke the lock and let Matt in.

Beckwith sneezed. "Weird smell in here, sir. I think it's coming from down there." He nodded at the door. "What do you reckon it is?"

"It looks like a cellar. Never mind that for now. Let's get Bella out of here."

They found her cowering behind the front door. The moment she saw Matt, she ran into his arms. "I thought he was going to kill me. I had no idea he was so dangerous. He's mad! Please, I have to leave here. I need to see Olly."

Matt nodded at Beckwith. "Take her out to Lily. We'll have a look round."

Matt made straight for the cellar. It was large, dank, and dark. He could make out a large bench with chains hanging from each corner. There was also what looked like dried blood covering the floor.

"Beckwith!" he shouted.

The DC was standing on the bottom step. "Backup are here, sir! We sent out photos of Turner. They're all set up at the station, just waiting for a call. Plus, we've got things organised in case he returns here. Lily has gone with Bella. She'll take her to a doctor and then get her to make a statement."

Matt was kicking at sheets of tarpaulin that lay scattered across the floor. His foot hit something soft, and he winced. "I think I've found Nolan." He took a pair of gloves from his pocket, put them on and carefully moved the covering to one side, revealing Robert Nolan's body. "He must have followed Bella up here. Poor man, a bullet through the neck from the look of him. Forensics will have a field day with this little lot. Look at the wall over there. Everything you need for a do-it-yourself torture chamber."

"What d'you reckon he's done with the women, sir?"

"They could be anywhere. Buried in the garden, bricked up behind a wall — who knows?"

* * *

Trusting Bella was a risk Mark was prepared to take. His farmhouse was miles from the nearest village on the edge of open moorland, and he'd locked up tight. Two of his nearest neighbours were abroad and the third was an elderly woman. Even if she did escape, Bella had no idea where she was, and wouldn't get far. Did he believe her soft words? He wanted to. The others had done nothing but whine and complain, so she was a refreshing change. She'd said she wanted them to be friends. He wanted it to be true. Perhaps it was, she was vulnerable and alone. Now she was his prisoner and reliant on him for everything. He'd chosen well. As he considered things, the more he realised that she really was the one.

It was several miles to Marsden where the nearest supermarket was. He'd get enough supplies for the next few days. He didn't want to go out again. He needed to spend time with Bella. They'd get to know each other better.

For the first time in years, Mark felt happy. Much more so than with the other two. Somehow, deep down, he'd known they weren't right. They had looked the part, but his love for them had not been reciprocated. Bella was different.

Walking towards the store, he passed a newsagent. The headline on the boards outside read: 'Police closing in on child abductor.' He laughed, he couldn't help it. They were wrong. But there was no room for complacency. He had to tread carefully, give nothing away. He'd been meticulous so far.

He wandered around the supermarket, humming to himself. Things had not been this good in months. He got everything he needed and headed to the checkout. It was then that he realised something was wrong.

* * *

After a quick scuffle, Mark Turner was apprehended. He barely put up any resistance. During the fifteen minutes or so it had taken him to do his shopping, the supermarket had been emptied, and plain-clothes officers had taken the shoppers' places. He'd been so wrapped up in his thoughts, he hadn't noticed.

"This is down to that scheming bitch!" he spat at the officer who handcuffed him. "She did this! But she won't get away with it. I'll have her, you'll see!" He could not understand what had gone wrong. The questions in his head made him dizzy. He was good at this, up until now, faultless. What had happened?

* * *

"We've got him, sir. Food shopping in Marsden, bold as brass. They've taken him to Huddersfield but he hasn't said a word," Lily said.

Matt felt a rush of relief. Forensics were well under way with their search of the farmhouse. He and Lily were standing in the cellar.

"No sign of Caroline and Anita," Lily said. "Bella told me that Turner had a wife. Her name was Kitty. She probably went the way of the other two. Bella is okay. The drugs he gave her won't do her any lasting harm. She had the wit to keep her cool, and made out she was happy to be there. That probably saved her life. She wouldn't have kept it up, though, not for long."

"No, she wouldn't, because Turner is a killer. He would have found some reason to incarcerate her in that cellar and do his worst."

Lily shuddered. "Bella knew him as James, not Doug. As far as she was concerned, he was her contact in the programme. You were right about that. Bella never suspected that he was a fake. It was him who took her to the prison in York. She had no idea that he was using a false name, or that he'd ever worked with Nolan."

"Like I said, clever. He made her believe she was being protected. He kept her isolated from everything and everyone she had ever known, so he could strike at will."

Lily looked at him. "Have we finished here, sir? This place is making me feel queasy."

A voice boomed down from the top of the cellar steps. "DI Brindle! Great job you've done. Now we've got him, we can't stop the bastard talking." It was Dyson. The stone steps were steep and worn with age, and he trod gingerly.

"Mad as a box of frogs, he is. He's admitted to the lot, including being our 'Mr Apology' and killing the so-called randoms. Apparently the stamps on the arms were part of some ritual. They were his way of saying sorry for taking their lives. Each woman had a special colour. Caroline was green, Anita red and Bella blue. God knows why. Like I said — bonkers."

Lily looked up at him. "Did he say anything about that cigarette end, sir? We were almost thrown off the scent there."

"He wanted us to blame Chalker. Wouldn't say where he got it from though. Don't think he can remember, to be honest. We're getting his DNA matched with what was taken from under Agnes Harvey's fingernails. That and his confession will nail the bugger for good."

They heard a voice calling down from the kitchen. "I think we may have found your missing women!"

Matt and Lily looked at each other. This was not going to be pleasant. Dyson led the way up to the kitchen. "Come on then, let's see what the bugger did with them."

The slate tiles on the kitchen floor had been taken up and were stacked in neat piles to one side.

"There. See? All that's left are three incomplete skeletons. Once we moved the car we found a pit in that outhouse. We will do tests, but I believe it was where he burned the bodies."

Lily grimaced. "So he killed his wife too. If it's okay with you, I'll wait outside. I've seen and heard enough. This is a dreadful place!"

Matt followed her out. "I'll speak to Bella later, and find out what she plans to do now."

Lily nodded. "She told me she feels guilty about Dawson. She said some nasty things to him, apparently. I did explain that it's down to him and his obsession with her that her life was saved."

"That, and Chalker recognising 'doorstep man' as our Mr Apology. We would not have found her without the input from both of them."

"I still think Joel Dawson is creepy, though. I wouldn't want anyone following me around, taking photos."

Matt smiled. "Ah well. Saved the day this time."

Lily looked at him, head to one side. "Have you made a decision about the job, sir?"

"Yes, Lily, but more about that tomorrow. I want you and Talbot to come up to the house and do me a small favour."

Epilogue

"The idea is that when visitors come into this room, they learn something about the history of the house and the family." Matt waved a hand.

"Stick some posters on the wall," Dyson suggested.

"No. People won't read them. I've got a much better idea. We'll give them a place to sit down and something to watch."

Lily smiled. "Like a movie?"

Matt nodded. "A very short one, no more than ten minutes."

"So why are we here?" Dyson asked.

"Because the two of you are going to be in it."

Dyson turned to Lily. "Don't like the sound of this, love. He's going to dress us up in some outlandish period costume and make bloody fools of us."

"Not at all." Evelyn Brindle strode into the room holding up two coat hangers. One held a long woollen dress and brown pinafore, with a small white hat. On the other, a pair of satin breeches, a frock coat and a frilly shirt. This she handed to Dyson. "I have a wig and shoes to go with these. Be very careful with them, they are the genuine article. Walter actually wore that outfit. We have a portrait in the drawing room of him dressed in it."

"You want me to wear this lot?"

Matt smiled at him. "You will make a perfect Walter Brindle. He was something of a dandy — loved his clothes and his fine wine. All you have to do is put the clothes on, sit on that fancy chair, and read from these cards. I'll hold them up for you. Josh here will do the filming."

A young man waiting at the back of the room made a little bow.

"And me?" Lily asked. "What's my part in this charade?"

"Scullery maid!" Evelyn Brindle replied with relish. "Halfway through, you will enter and put fresh coals on the fire."

"How long is this reading?"

"Not long, Talbot. The idea is that the visitors will push a button on the wall, and that will start the film. You'll be in that chair, snoozing. When they press the button, you'll wake up, welcome them and talk about your day."

Dyson sighed. Resignedly, he took the clothes from Evelyn. "Okay. But there'll be a price to pay for this, lad. You. At the station Monday morning, all fresh, and ready to sort out your new team."

"I can live with that, Talbot. As for the team, I've already made my mind up. I'd like Lily and Beckwith, if it's alright with you?" He turned to Lily. "That okay? Fancy giving 'chalk and cheese' a go?"

THE END

Thank you for reading this book. If you enjoyed it please leave feedback on Amazon, and if there is anything we missed or you have a question about then please get in touch. The author and publishing team appreciate your feedback and time reading this book.

Our email is office@joffebooks.com

www.joffebooks.com

ALSO BY HELEN H. DURRANT

CALLADINE & BAYLISS MYSTERIES
DEAD WRONG
DEAD SILENT
DEAD LIST
DEAD LOST
DEAD & BURIED
DEAD NASTY
DEAD JEALOUS

DI GRECO
DARK MURDER
DARK HOUSES
DARK TRADE

DI MATT BRINDLE
HIS THIRD VICTIM

Made in the USA
Middletown, DE
06 November 2017